A RINGSIDE
ROMANCE

WORKING IT
CHRISTINE D'ABO

RIPTIDE
PUBLISHING

Riptide Publishing
PO Box 1537
Burnsville, NC 28714
www.riptidepublishing.com

Working It

Cover art: L.C. Chase, lcchase.com/design.htm
Editor: Delphine Dryden, delphinedryden.com/editing
Layout: L.C. Chase, lcchase.com/design.htm

ISBN: 978-1-62649-522-7

First edition
February, 2017

Also available in ebook:
ISBN: 978-1-62649-521-0

A RINGSIDE
ROMANCE

WORKING IT

CHRISTINE D'ABO

RIPTIDE
PUBLISHING

TABLE OF
CONTENTS

= CHAPTER =
ONE

Nolan hated mirrors. They were an unfortunate necessity for his morning routine—shaving, tying his tie, doing what he needed to fix his hair—but it was still strange to see himself, even after nearly two years of adjusting to the changes.

His sister, Tina, said nothing was different about him, he was the same old Nolan. She was sweet to say so, but he knew the truth.

Come on, get your act together.

He gave himself a moment and went through his anxiety checklist, ensuring he'd be able to keep himself in one piece. He hated having to do that, almost as much as he hated mirrors. Still, his therapist had been right about so many other things, he'd come to accept she knew what she was doing. He closed his eyes and tried to focus on his emotions. Yeah, he was nervous, worried about what people would think of him. It was a job interview, and he was underqualified for the position; that would raise questions he didn't want to answer. Only an idiot wouldn't be worried. He was also angry his life had taken such a horrible turn that he was forced to be in this position in the first place.

Nothing new, then.

Opening his eyes, he looked directly at himself as he turned on the water and let it flow over his hands, grounding him in the here and now. He took a deep breath, held it for a three count before letting it go.

"The water is warm from when I shaved a few moments ago. The running water sounds relax me and make me think of a river. The mirror needs cleaning. I need to remind Tina that I want to get a small water feature for the living room. It will help settle my mind in the morning . . ." He shook his head and gently directed his thoughts back to the present, to what his five senses told him. "I can smell the shaving cream, and maybe the fabric softener on this shirt. I can taste the mint from my toothpaste."

He held his hands there until his fingers started to prune. He took extra time to dry his hands, enjoying the feel and smell of the fresh towel. It hadn't been hard to convince Tina to switch fabric softeners, especially since he was paying for it. There was something to be said for the finer things.

Okay, the tie looked good, mostly straight. He adjusted it again and debated changing it one more time. No, damn it, he'd already wasted the better part of ten minutes picking this one out. It was fine.

Hair? He'd been growing it out in front since the accident, but still wasn't entirely used to it. A necessary evil. Knowing exactly what he would find, he lifted up the long fringe that covered the left side of his forehead. The scar had faded to a light pink, a jagged road running just below his hairline. It was the least horrific of his injuries, and yet he couldn't help but hate it the most. Nolan had never considered himself a particularly vain man, but he despised how the scar on his face opened him up to questions and comments, as if everyone felt entitled to information about his body now that it was so visibly flawed.

Oh my God, what happened?
Did it hurt?
You're lucky you didn't lose an eye.
Do you have other scars?

Not the sort of conversation he wanted to have with his family and friends, let alone complete strangers who didn't know the first thing about him.

The hair fell back into place, and he took another moment to ensure nothing looked off. If the people at Compass Technologies noticed, he'd have a polite response ready to go; he'd memorized quite a few. It helped with the stress and prevented his anxiety from overwhelming him.

In theory at least.

He hated interviews. Even before the accident, he'd sucked at them on a good day, and he had a feeling that today would be anything but good. Nerves and doubts were more his enemy than the other applicants. At least he assumed he was the only neurotic, panic-prone candidate they were meeting with this afternoon. His résumé spoke for itself, as did his references; none of that would matter, though, if he broke out into a full-blown anxiety attack the moment he walked into the office.

No, he wasn't going to let that happen today. Not this time.

Yes, his life had been challenging over the past two years, but that didn't mean he had to let what had happened control his future. He'd fought through physiotherapy, got his broken body working again, and that alone proved how strong he was. Didn't it?

Damn straight it did.

Shaking his head, Nolan let out a breath and marched out of the tiny powder room. *Ready or not, here I go.*

"Let me see."

So not ready . . .

Groaning, he turned and faced his big sister. "I do know how to dress myself. I've been doing it on my own for years now."

Tina snorted before proceeding to loosen his tie. He ducked her attempts to run her fingers through his hair.

"Come here. You look like an uptight asshole."

"I *am* an uptight asshole. Will you fuck off?" He stepped past her and did his best to avoid her grabbing hands. "I'm going to be late."

"No, you're not. You're going to be a half hour early because you're always early."

"I won't be if you don't stop picking."

"I'm just making sure you look your best. I want you out of here."

As much as she bitched about him crashing at her apartment, he knew she didn't mind. Well, maybe she did a little. Okay, probably more than a little. "I told you I can get my own place anytime. I have savings and am more than capable."

"Not until you know if you have a job. I promised you could stay here until then, and I keep my promises." She stepped in front of him as he finished slipping his dress shoes on. "Let me see."

This would go far faster if he gave in to her prodding. Nolan straightened up and held his arms out slightly. "Fine. Have at me."

The grin Tina gave him was positively satanic. Her fingers raked through his fringe and she brushed some lint from the back of his blazer. "You look good. Really good. Maybe you'll find a hot guy to go with your new job."

"Thank you. I don't have the job yet, and I doubt they offer hot men as a signing bonus."

Tina laughed. "That would be an interesting contract negotiation."

His nerves gave way to a chuckle of his own. "Can you imagine? Now *that* would bring on a panic attack. Thankfully, that won't happen. Can I go now?"

"Yes." She pulled him into a hug, giving him an extra squeeze when he finally reciprocated. "Are you doing okay?"

He should have expected the question; his own poor attempt at a joke had given her the opening she was looking for. This was his first interview since his accident . . . and since the subsequent mental meltdown at work when he'd tried to go back to his previous job. He knew the possibility of an attack was weighing as heavily on her mind as it was with him. "I'm good. Took my pills, had a good sleep, and my leg doesn't hurt at all. Only mildly freaked out right now."

"On a scale of one to ten?"

"Four."

She pulled back and gave him The Look.

"Okay, a six. But I don't think it'll get any worse. Believe it or not, I'm looking forward to trying this."

It was weird how his emotions could be a chaotic mix of excitement and nerves while his body kept urging him to pee. *Stupid body.*

Tina stepped back, giving his hand one final squeeze before she let go. "You have my number. If there's a problem, call me, and I'll come get you."

"I'm twenty-six, not a child."

"Nolan, don't be like that."

He knew she was only trying to help. Tina and he were the closest in age, far younger than their three older brothers. Over the years they'd learned to look out for one another. Despite working full-time and with a busy volunteer schedule, Tina had spent a part of every day with him after the accident, helping him get back on his feet. Literally at first, then figuratively. Without her, Nolan knew his recovery would have taken a lot longer. She might be a pain in the ass, but she loved him. And he loved her more than anyone or anything in the world.

He lowered his chin and sighed. "Sorry. I guess I'm more nervous than I realized. I'll call you if I have any problems."

"Thank you. Or text me, and I'll send you goofy gifs or something. Now, go knock 'em dead."

"I think they frown upon that at job interviews." He gave her a quick kiss to the cheek before making his escape. If he didn't get on the road now, he would miss his ride, and then he really would be late.

His Uber driver was pleasant, on time, and more importantly a nontalker, making the drive to Toronto's downtown core uneventful. It gave Nolan a few moments to mentally prepare. It had been a while since he'd interviewed for a position, let alone something that wasn't in his field of expertise. His career history would inevitably lead to questions about why he wanted to change paths. That was something he would avoid going into detail about if at all possible.

Looking down, he caught himself rubbing at his thigh, and lifted his hand.

"Hey, we're here." His driver double-parked, not giving Nolan much time to get his things together before people started honking. Fortunately, his leg was cooperative today—painful, but not cramping.

"Thanks." Nolan stepped out of the car, shut the door, and made his way to the busy sidewalk before he happened to glance up at the building he hoped would soon be his place of employment. He stopped cold. The familiar tightening in his chest began as his thigh throbbed. Shit, no, this couldn't happen now. He could fall apart *after* the interview. Hell, he could puke in the washroom the moment it was done, but not a second sooner.

Get your ass moving!

His feet stayed planted.

Fuck.

Reaching into his pocket, he wrapped his fingers around his phone. Tina was only a text away if he needed her. Not that he would give in to the impulse.

Closing his eyes, he focused on the sounds around him, taking a moment to identify several individual elements before moving on to the smells. Exhaust, street meat, and something that smelled strangely of urine. *Wonderful.* But grounding. When he finally opened his eyes, the colors of the bustling downtown seemed momentarily sharper. Regardless of how he did this morning, the world would keep turning and he'd keep going.

He took a step toward the building. Then another. One foot in front of the other until he made his way through the front door and to the security desk.

Don't forget to smile. Of course it was Tina's voice in his head. The smile felt foreign on his face, and his lips trembled from the strain. It worked, though, helping him push through the panic to speak to the woman behind the counter. "Hello. I'm Nolan Carmichael, and I have an interview at ten with Compass Technologies."

She barely looked at him as she went through her list. "Yup, there you are. Take this badge and go up to the fourteenth floor. Swipe it through the card reader first, then select the floor number. Make sure to return it here when you're done." She then smiled at him without making eye contact. "Good luck."

That wasn't the least bit reassuring. "Thanks."

After a short battle with the security badge, the elevator doors closed and the carriage flew up. His stomach fell somewhere around his feet from the speed, only to come slamming back into place when it stopped. By the time he reached his destination and stepped off the elevator into a tastefully decorated front-office area, he was ready to go back home to bed. *Why did existing have to be so hard some days?*

"Welcome to Compass. How may I help you?" The gray-haired woman behind the reception desk smiled pleasantly enough. "Interview today?"

"Yes. Nolan Carmichael."

She ticked his name off. "Wonderful. They're running a bit late. Please have a seat with the others and I'll let you know when they're ready for you."

"Thanks."

The seating area she'd directed him to held eight other hopeful candidates. Most were women, but there was one other man, which helped relieve some of Nolan's tension. He'd assumed there would be far fewer male executive assistants than female, so it was nice to know he wasn't the only one in the applicant pool.

All he had to do now was wait.

No problem at *all*.

His nerves crept up on him as time crawled forward. One older woman was called in, then the other man. The wall clock's second hand ticked steadily forward, and constantly drew his attention. Damn it, this was worse than he'd thought it would be. And to top things off, he now really did have to pee. He should do that. Nothing worse than squirming his way through an interview. Or worse, being so nervous that he pissed himself.

He got to his feet so quickly he drew the attention of the remaining interviewees. *Shit.* Ignoring them, he strode over to the receptionist. "Hi. I'm sorry. Do I have time to use the washroom?"

She peeked at her computer screen. "Yes. There's one person ahead of you still. It's down the hall and on your left."

"Thank you."

Thankfully, the bathroom was empty. Granite countertops lined the wall, and held a long trough-style sink. Nolan used the urinal and washed his hands, then took a moment to splash water on his face, close his eyes, and run through his breathing techniques. *Get a handle on yourself. It's just a job interview.*

For a position he'd never held before. One that would make the interviewers ask why he was settling for a lower salary range, less room for advancement . . .

No, nothing to worry about at all.

Closing his eyes, he focused on his breathing and ignored the pain that was creeping up his thigh toward his hip. *In and out. Nice and deep. Relax.* He wasn't in a full-blown anxiety attack yet, so he knew he still had a chance to get a grip. The fan in the bathroom hummed softly in the background, and he latched on to that. It wasn't the same as running water, but it was better than turning his hands into prunes before walking into a social situation.

He counted backward from one hundred in his head; around sixty-three, he felt he could finally breathe normally again.

Okay, he could do this.

His leg still throbbed, no doubt from forcing himself to walk without his slight limp. Being slightly off-balance was probably the reason he caught sight of his profile in the mirror beside the sink.

Nolan knew better than to look—he'd practically trained himself not to—but his eyes focused on to his image and refused to move away.

He'd lost so much weight in the past two years his suit hung on him, giving him the appearance of a kid who'd put on his dad's coat. He could live with that. It was his face that still looked like an imposter's.

The surgeons had done an amazing job with his reconstruction. No one who hadn't spent day in and day out with him would even notice the slight change of his nose's shape, or the way his left eyebrow didn't quite curve the right way. But Nolan found his reflection eerie, so close to correct that it was somehow worse than if he'd appeared as an entirely different person. How could he be himself, know himself, and still not recognize the man in the mirror?

He ran a finger along the side of his jaw where the break had been and pressed against the cheek and into the hole that should have been filled by a tooth. That would be the first thing he'd get fixed the moment he had dental benefits.

Nolan startled as the door pushed open and a man strode past him. It was easy to let his eyes follow the newcomer, partially because he was all energy and motion, walking with a sense of purpose, but mostly because Nolan didn't want to look any longer at the flawed restoration project he'd become. The lingering scent of the man's cologne wrapped around Nolan, making him wonder if the guy's face was as attractive as the back of his head.

Wait a minute. What the hell am I doing?

Nolan's body froze, and he was helpless to do anything but watch the man in the mirror as he made his way from the urinals to the sink. *Shit, shit, shit, look away. Close your eyes. Stop. Looking!* Somehow he managed to tear his gaze away before the man finished and made his way to the opposite mirror to fix his tie. As long as Nolan didn't bring any undue attention on himself, everything would be fine. The man moved, and Nolan was staring at him once more. God, he was far too good-looking.

Nolan had been lucky enough to come out to his friends and family early in life. While some of his brothers had teased him, they'd always accepted him for who he was. But Nolan wasn't naïve enough to think that everyone was as accommodating of his sexuality, especially strangers going about their business in the men's room. And if he went around ogling hot guys in the men's room, people were likely to draw the obvious conclusion.

"Something I can help you with?"

It took Nolan's brain a second to realize that the deep rumbling voice had come from the man beside him. "Pardon?"

"You were staring." The man's brown eyes locked onto his in the mirror as he finished washing his hands.

Damn. "Sorry." Wonderful, nothing like being a lecherous ass at a job interview. "I'm here for an interview and apparently I'm a bit nervous."

The man frowned, causing lines to crease his forehead and cheeks. "The secretary pool?"

"Executive assistant." He hated the position being called *secretary* as much as he imagined the women did. "And yes."

"That's unusual. For a man."

"Not really. Though I have to admit the competition from the ladies is steep, especially at a company of this caliber."

The other man softly grunted. "You enjoy your job?"

To his surprise, Nolan found himself relaxing. "I don't know. It will be my first time in the position if I manage to get hired."

"We don't normally hire inexperienced people."

Nolan shrugged. "I'm not inexperienced. I've had a recent . . . career change and Compass seems to offer a compatible opportunity for my skill set."

The stranger looked at him, and Nolan felt a blush begin to creep up his cheeks. The man wore his clearly expensive suit to perfection. His expertly cut brown hair was nearly the same shade of brown as his eyes. He was only a bit taller than Nolan's six feet, but his broad shoulders and chest were far more expansive than Nolan's.

For a fleeting moment, Nolan imagined what it would be like to be wrapped up in those arms and to kiss along that chiseled jaw. Swallowing hard, he tore his gaze away once more. "I better get back. I don't want to be late."

If the man acknowledged that, Nolan didn't wait around to see. The air in the hallway felt a hundred degrees cooler the moment he stepped out. Shit, what the hell had just happened in there? He never let himself get that overwhelmed by another person. At least the throat-squeezing anxiety had lessened.

The receptionist caught his attention as he came close. "They're ready for you, Mr. Carmichael."

Oh thank God. At least he could get through this now and get home. He needed a bath, a beer, and a good book. "Thank you."

The conference room was down a short corridor, and inside were three women. The tallest of the trio stood and held out her hand. "Hi there. I'm Nancy Holmes from HR. This is Janice Weinstein, the manager of our support team, and Nikki Jones, the team lead. Please have a seat."

Nolan unbuttoned his jacket and sat opposite the group. "Thank you."

Janice picked up his résumé from the top of the stack of papers. "Your work history is very impressive, Mr. Carmichael."

"Please, call me Nolan. And thank you."

"Though you don't have any assistant experience." The smile Janice gave him didn't reach her eyes. *Oh no, that wasn't good.* "First thing I want to do is let you know about our process. We'll give you a moment to tell us about your work history, then we'll ask you a series of behavior-based questions. There's no right or wrong answer with those. We simply want to get a feel for who you are as a person and if you'll be a good fit for our team."

He *hated* behavioral questions. It always came down to whether his answers were less obnoxious than everyone else's, and he knew he could be a smart-ass at times. "Excellent. I'm looking forward to it."

Janice glanced at her colleagues and nodded. "Please tell us a bit about your work history and why you're making the change from corporate trainer to administrative support."

He opened his mouth to speak, when a loud knock on the door cut him off. Nancy cringed as she stood. "Sorry. One second."

Nolan wasn't certain who was more surprised, him or the trio of women, when the handsome man from the bathroom walked into the room.

"Mr. Anderson." Nancy took a step back. "We were just conducting an interview. Is there something I can help you with?"

Mr. Anderson walked passed Nancy and over to the table where they were sitting. Without looking at anyone, he took Nolan's résumé from Janice's grasp and read through it. While the women were silently shouting thoughts at one another about what the hell was happening—and really, they needed to work on their body language—Nolan flicked his gaze between Mr. Anderson and the door. Because there was no logical reason for this guy to burst into the interview unless he was about to call security and have Nolan removed for creepy bathroom behavior.

That might have been farfetched, but Nolan's anxiety discarded any more innocuous explanation. His mind settled on the worst-case scenario and told him he'd been discounted before he'd even had the chance to make a bid for the position.

Shit.

After an eternity, Mr. Anderson set the résumé down and turned his laser stare on Nolan.

"Are you single?"

"Mr. Anderson, you can't ask that—"

"Yes, I am." Assuming the interview was over and Mr. Anderson was just asking random questions to stall for time to let security arrive, Nolan got to his feet and buttoned his jacket, ready to go along peaceably. To his surprise, Anderson's queries turned more direct.

"Do you have any issues working long hours? Coming in on a moment's notice? Redoing reports more than once if they don't meet my requirements? Dealing with people I can't be bothered to talk to?"

Nancy coughed. "Sir, are you looking for a secretary?"

"Executive assistant," Mr. Anderson answered without looking away from Nolan.

He felt his face heat, but he refused to break eye contact. "No, I don't have issues with any of that. Though if you need me to do a report more than twice, I would want your expectations clarified so I could make sure it wouldn't happen again. I might not have a lot of experience as an assistant, but I was always good with paperwork in my previous job and I'm a fast learner. If I don't know how to do something, I figure it out and master it."

Mr. Anderson hit the side of his thigh with his open palm. "Your evaluation period is three months. I can fire you for any reason in that time."

What? "I understand." *Liar! You don't have a clue what's going on here.* It finally dawned on Nolan that he was not, in fact, about to be thrown out on his ear.

"Monday morning, 7 a.m. I expect you at my office." Mr. Anderson tossed a glare at Nancy. "See that the paperwork is done." As quickly as he arrived, Mr. Anderson was gone.

Nolan looked at the women, who were staring at him, shocked. He cleared his throat. "I know I was here, because my feet haven't moved, but would one of you mind telling me what just happened?"

"That was Mr. Zachary Anderson." Nancy spoke with a mix of awe and something that could have been mistaken for lust.

"I got that. But who *is* he?"

Janice rolled her eyes. "You've applied for a job at Compass and you don't know who the senior management team is?"

"Well the CEO is Samantha Rollins, but I wasn't familiar with the others. I wasn't expecting to be railroaded in an interview."

Nancy made a clicking noise. "Yeah, he does that. Mr. Anderson is the CTO. He's in charge of all technology decisions at Compass. He's basically the third most powerful man in the company, and the most difficult of all our executives to work with. We'd given up trying to find him an assistant after the last four either quit or he fired them."

Nolan's knees got a bit weak. "Oh."

"And he's your new boss." She held out her hand. "Welcome to Compass, Nolan. God help you."

= CHAPTER = TWO

Zack ignored the stares of the employees in the lobby as he strode through toward the exit. He needed to get out of the building for a few hours and get a drink or else he was going to lose his mind. Maybe it was already too late for that, given the odd way he'd been acting all day.

He'd hired himself an assistant this morning.

Again.

He *hated* having an assistant. Hated being micromanaged, having the need for that person to be involved in his business all the time. It was worse than when he'd lived at home and had to declare his comings and goings to his parents.

What had possessed him to follow Nolan into the interview room after their brief encounter in the men's room, he still wasn't sure. The nerves radiating off Nolan in the bathroom were practically visible; he was not at all the type of person Zack wanted to have to deal with on a daily basis. He didn't have time to coddle a new hire, nor did he think the poorly dressed, almost frail-looking man would necessarily be able to handle his *moods*.

It was a horrible idea.

He should probably tell HR to find Nolan another executive or team to work with and save them both a world of headaches.

Yes, he'd do that when he got back.

But first he needed to see Max.

It would have made sense for him to take his car, given how far away Frantic was, but he needed to stretch his legs and taking transit worked for him. Him behind the wheel, feeling the way he was, wouldn't end well.

He hated days when his brain seemed out of sync with his body. Thoughts banging up against one another, too many projects vying for his attention, things he desperately wanted to make happen but had to stomp the brakes on because of *process*. Or the worst: having to be quiet when other people thought they knew better than he did. They usually didn't. It wasn't all arrogance that led him to that conclusion; it was years of being proven right time and time again. But he'd learned the hard way there were certain people you couldn't tell what to do and how to do it.

His boss being one of them.

He'd have to go to the gym after work, if for no other reason than to bleed off enough excess energy that he could sleep later. Really, it would do him a world of good to hit something.

It took him nearly forty minutes and two buses to get to Max's bar. He didn't need to check to see if Max would be there. It was nearly four, and his friend was always the one to open the club. The door was locked, so Zack pulled out his phone.

Let me in.

There was a minute-long pause before Max's response popped up. *Why are you here?*

To bug you. Let me in.

Go back to work.

Asshole.

Zack had barely pressed Send when the door's lock clicked and Max opened the door. "Why do you torture me?"

"Because I'm your friend and business partner."

Max rolled his eyes and walked away. "Still an asshole."

Frantic was currently empty, but Zack knew that in a short time staff would start arriving and prep would be underway for Friday night's inevitable crowd. "We need to talk about Ringside."

Max's groan echoed in the empty dance area. "We need a drink, then."

"Beer?"

"I'm not giving you anything good. That's for paying customers."

"I pay."

"Not in the last five years you haven't. Cheap prick." Max pulled two bottles from beneath the bar and cracked the caps off before sliding one to Zack. "What's going on with the gym?"

"I was going to ask you. Any word on those investors of yours?" The beer was cold and slid easily down his throat as he took several long pulls. "I need some good news today."

Max grinned as he shook his head. "So impatient for a business guy."

"I'm used to things happening on my timetable, not some mysterious venture capitalist who I don't even know is worth his word."

They'd been working on getting their childhood sanctuary up and running again far too long for Zack to not be impatient. Starting Frantic had been Max's dream, one Zack had helped him with from square one; reopening Ringside Boxing was Zack's, and he'd be damned if anything would stop him.

Max downed his beer far too quickly and tossed the bottle in a recycling bin. "My investor said he was looking to find some new LGBTQ businesses to invest in around Toronto. He's got connections, and Ringside has solid PR opportunities given what you've planned. The teen programs are also great advertising to have at schools. We'll make this happen."

"We better."

Max frowned. "What the hell crawled up your ass and died? You're more of a jerk than usual."

"Nothing."

"Bullshit. You look like you're ready to run a marathon or take on crime or something."

Max had been his closest friend since they'd met at the original Ringside gym when they were both sixteen. If anyone could tell when Zack was on edge, it was Max. "I just don't want anything to screw this up."

Along with their friend Eli, the three of them had spent the better part of their high school years as part of an LGBTQ teen-outreach program at Ringside. Max and Eli had used boxing as a way to develop their self-confidence and learn how to defend themselves. Zack had never lacked either of those skills, even at a young age. No, he'd used his workouts at Ringside as a way to funnel the buildup of emotions that constantly swirled inside him. Sparring in the ring had helped him learn how to direct that charge outward and stop himself from losing his shit on his parents, friends, and teachers.

Russel Kinson, the previous owner of Ringside, had done so much for so many people over the years that a piece of Zack had broken when he'd died and the place shut down. How many more kids and troubled youth could have been helped in the intervening years? How many more like himself, Max, and Eli?

Despite what everyone thought about him, working at Compass Technologies wasn't his life's goal. It was little more than a means to an end. Within the next year or two, he wanted to walk away from all things technology and spend his days helping people the way Russel had helped him.

Max started taking clean mugs from the wash tray and stacking them in the bar. "So what happened at work to get you all riled up? That boss of yours on the warpath again?"

The image of a too skinny and pale Nolan flashed through his head. "I hired an assistant."

"Jesus. I thought you swore you wouldn't do that to someone else again?"

"It was an impulsive hire."

"*Nooo.* You'd never do anything like that."

Zack growled. "He's different from the others, though I doubt that I'll keep him. Better to have HR rehome him before I chew his head off."

"Whoa, back up. You hired a *male* assistant?" Max leaned over the bar and grinned. "Is he cute?"

"He's way too thin and not even remotely my type." God, he couldn't imagine anyone further away from the sort of man he was attracted to; Nolan lacked confidence, didn't have that edge Zack looked for in a partner. He couldn't imagine what it would be like to have sex with someone like that. He liked it rough, fucked the same way he fought both in the ring and in business. Nolan would no doubt be overwhelmed by everything Zack would want. Not that he was into any kinky shit, but he liked things hard and fast: fucking, not making love.

Max clicked his tongue. "Huh."

"What?"

"Nothing. You're just full of surprises."

Zack's cell chose that moment to sound off. "Shit."

"What?"

The notification tone he'd specifically assigned to Samantha Rollins told him who'd emailed without his having to look at the name. *Problem with the Korean shipment of the network appliance.* "I have to head back to the office."

"Something wrong?"

"Nothing I can't handle." He was the best at putting out fires, a skill set Samantha had taken advantage of for the past three years. "But I won't be stopping in tonight."

"Good, that'll leave some of the hot guys for me for a change."

"Like you've ever had a problem with that before."

"I take it your assistant won't be with you this evening?"

"No. Starts Monday."

"That's good. Don't want to burn the poor boy out before he's even gotten his feet wet. I'll let you know as soon as I hear from my investor and I can set up a meeting between the two of you."

"Thanks. I'll talk to you next week about it."

Traffic had kicked up considerably since his arrival, as people began their treks home from work. The buses and subway would be packed, but faster than a taxi. Still, Zack flagged the closest one down, not wanting to deal with the off and on and jostling of bodies.

The moment the door closed and the cab pulled into traffic, Zack knew it had been a mistake. Being stuck in the backseat with nothing but his thoughts was liable to drive him nuts. He pulled out his phone and read through Samantha's email, ensuring he had a grasp on the situation. Someone else had screwed up, and she needed him to smooth things over. Typical and easy enough to sort through.

A new email popped onto the top of the screen from Nancy in HR. *New Hire Confirmation: Nolan Carmichael*

Nothing was set in stone yet. He could easily brush the entire incident off and Nancy would no doubt find another role for the man, or at the very least let him down easy. Zack had no illusions about how difficult he was to work with. Nolan seemed like a decent sort, and shouldn't be subjected to him.

No one should.

He hit Reply, his thumbs poised over the screen keyboard to tell her never mind, that it had been a horrible idea.

And yet.

God, he couldn't put his finger on it, but there'd been something about Nolan—about the way he'd looked in the bathroom, scared and lost—that spoke to him. Zack had been that way once, back before Russel had taken him in at the gym as part of his program. Nolan might not exude the same confidence Zack had, but neither had he shied away from him once Zack hijacked the interview. Nolan had held his gaze, given concise answers to his questions, and didn't once look as though Zack was the Devil incarnate.

That was more than he could say for most employees at Compass.

Running on the same impulse that seemed to have been at his back all day, he typed out a terse acknowledgment. Nolan Carmichael, for good or ill, would start Monday morning as his new assistant.

Zack could only hope he wasn't making a mistake. For both their sakes.

CHAPTER THREE

B y the time Sunday afternoon rolled around, Nolan was exhausted. Background checks, reference calls, paperwork that demanded reading and signatures had filled the time from nearly the moment Zack had left the interview room on Friday. In between doing the various things he needed to for Compass, he'd called his parents to let them know the good news. Tina had been so excited she'd even taken him out for supper last night, though he really didn't remember much of the food.

His head had been rolling through the series of events that had led him to this moment. What had Zachary Anderson seen in him to warrant such an impulsive hire? Sure, Nolan was skilled, but there'd been nothing in their brief encounter, either in the bathroom or in the interview itself, that should have set this in motion.

Had there?

Nancy from HR currently sat across from him at the Starbucks they'd agreed to meet at to go over the last-minute details. He'd tried to tell her it wasn't necessary, but he got the impression that HR did things differently for high-ranking executives, including how their hires were dealt with. His coffee mug sat untouched between them as he read through what must have been the most boring document in the history of HR manuals. He only looked up when she started to chuckle. "What?"

Nancy was devoid of makeup and dressed far more casually than during the interview. The natural look was stunning and gave her a glow that hadn't come through when they'd first met. Especially when she smiled. "You. I get the feeling you're completely overwhelmed by everything that's going on."

There was the understatement of the century. "I haven't slept through the night since the interview." Setting the papers down, Nolan leaned forward. Despite everything he'd read, there was one question he knew he wouldn't find the answer to there. "Is he really that horrible?"

Nancy's smile faltered. "Zack can be . . . demanding."

"You're being polite. I can't have you be polite. I need to know *exactly* what I'm going to be walking into tomorrow morning so I don't have a panic attack. Because, believe me, my imagination is far worse than whatever the truth probably is."

Nancy shook her head. "Okay. Zack can be a demanding *asshole*. He's hard to get to know, shows little concern for anyone or anything outside of the company. In the eight years I've worked at Compass, I haven't heard anyone say that they like him. Respect his work ethic, admire his ability to solve problems and get things done, stand in awe of his seemingly boundless energy. But not actually like him. His previous assistants have all quit or been fired within two weeks of starting. In their exit interviews they said Zack had trouble delegating and rarely gave out praise, which a lot of people have problems with."

The blunt description of his new boss should have freaked him out. The long-familiar invisible fingers should be squeezing his chest and his stomach should be churning. Nolan frowned and looked down at his body. Nope, still not freaking out.

Huh. Weird. "That's good to know."

Nancy leaned back against her chair. "Any other questions?"

He picked up his contract, the last document she'd handed over to him. "So once I sign this I'm all set?"

"Yes. I know you need this job, and Compass really is a great company. If things don't work out with this position, don't quit. Even though we found a new hire for our team, there's still room in the company, and I can find you a position somewhere. Please don't let Zack scare you away. We'll make this work. Okay?"

There was something about the way she spoke that made Nolan suspect he wasn't the first person she'd said that to. "I don't like to make promises I can't keep, but I will do my best. If things don't work out between me and Mr. Anderson, I'll at least do you the courtesy of letting you know as quickly as I can."

Her shoulders relaxed. "That's all I can ask."

This was it. Nolan could either set the contract down and walk away—and if he did, he had the impression Nancy wouldn't think any less of him—or he could sign it knowing exactly how difficult his boss would be. "Do you have a pen?"

Nancy grinned as she rescued her pen from beneath the papers. "I'm so glad. I get the feeling you and I will get along wonderfully."

"Of that I have no doubt." He finished signing with a little flourish. "There. All done but the crying." He looked up wide-eyed. "I'm allowed to cry, right? Birthdays, babies, retirements? I become an emotional mess when it comes to those things, and I'm secure enough in my masculinity to show it."

"That'll be nice for a change. Janice is a robot, I swear. The woman barely smiles!"

"No robots here. I'm even up for sappy movies at the drop of a hat."

Nancy rocked her mug between her hands, a smile still tugging at her lips. "May I ask you a personal question? Off the record and in no way going to impact your position."

Those questions rarely went well. "About?"

When she started to blush he realized what she was going to ask before the words came out of her mouth. "Are you gay?"

"I am." He smiled and wanted to laugh at the cute look of disappointment on her face. "Is that a problem, or did I burst a bubble?"

She rolled her eyes, but smiled nonetheless. "No, not a problem and maybe a small bubble." She held up her thumb and forefinger. "About this big."

"Sorry about that. Knew I was gay from about eight on, when I dreamed about watching Disney films and wanting to be the one to kiss the prince. But I'd love to officially court you as my work wife. I was always jealous of some coworkers at my last company who had that sort of relationship."

"You'd have to bring me flowers." Her smile widened into a grin. "And I know this excellent bakery that makes the best cupcakes. More than happy to offer comfort and bribes with them."

"See, I knew we'd be a good match. You can help calm me down when I get in a frenzy."

Nancy's smile slipped. "That's twice you've mentioned panic. Is that really a big issue for you?"

Shit, he hadn't intended to let people know about his challenges for fear of it counting against him in the interview process. While he and Nancy clearly had a good rapport, she was still bound to Compass in a professional capacity.

"Hey." She covered his hand with hers. "I promise it's not an issue. I just want to make sure that if you need help, I do the right thing. I have a sister who worked through some tough anxiety when she was a teen. It can be brutal, and I know everyone is a bit different."

The knot in his shoulders relaxed slightly. "My sister has helped me quite a bit too since my accident."

He could go into a long explanation of what had happened. He could talk about the screams that had filled the car as he'd lost control, sending him and his passengers into the ditch. But that wasn't information that would help Nancy. If anything, it would scare the shit out of her.

The silence stretched on, and Nancy squirmed in her seat. "I'm sorry. You don't have to say anything."

"It's not that." Despite his therapist encouraging him to talk to people about what had happened, he hadn't said much to anyone outside of family. He shook his head and let his gaze wander. "They told me that what I experience is closer to PTSD than anxiety. The results are the same though. I get overwhelmed, panicked. Breathing can become difficult, and I passed out once. That was a year ago and the reason I left my job in training. I just couldn't . . ."

"I'm sorry."

"Thanks. If anything happens, I normally just need to know that someone is there. I'm usually okay with a gentle touch, but not anything else. And I need a quiet spot. No gawkers wondering who the freak is."

"You're not a freak. If anything, I get the impression you're a much stronger man than most people realize."

Nolan swallowed down the unexpected tightness in his throat. "You're not supposed to make me cry before I've even officially started work."

"Well then I owe you a cupcake."

"I look forward to it."

Maybe working at Compass wasn't going to be as terrifying as he'd initially thought.

Going through a serious health scare, like what had resulted from his accident, had made it difficult for Nolan to see past the end of his nose. Nothing planned six months to a year in the future mattered if you couldn't get to the bathroom in the next five minutes because your leg was crippled. Signing a contract, going over insurance details, discussing vacation time, had reminded Nolan that he wasn't stuck in the short term anymore; the realization was equal parts liberating and terrifying. He'd gone home after his meeting with Nancy and proceeded to get himself organized for his first day on the job. Having everything ready to go made Monday morning that much easier.

His conversation with Nancy had given him a sense of rightness that had been missing from his life for a while now. It was refreshing to talk to someone who didn't treat him with kid gloves the entire time. Maybe working with Mr. Anderson would be the change he needed: someone who wouldn't walk on egg shells, who would crack the whip if he was starting to slack.

As long as Nolan didn't fall apart, everything would be good.

Nancy was waiting for him at the security desk when he arrived, a chocolate cupcake in hand. "Good morning." She set the treat on top of a security access card and handed it to him. "I try to keep my promises."

"We are going to have a great working relationship." He took a bite and moaned. "I love you. Marry me."

"Of course. So, are you ready for this?"

No. Not even a little. "I can't wait to get started."

"You need to work on your lying skills."

"I'll add that to my training plan."

She laughed as she led him toward the elevators. "Okay, let me give you the quick rundown. Mr. Anderson is normally here early and stays late. Yes, you will need to stay a bit later some days, but don't let him ruin your life. If he's determined to stay and you need to leave, just go. I know he wanted you to come to his office this morning, but later today you'll also need to do the normal HR stuff. Orientation, health and safety training. The usual."

Nolan's head began to pound in time with the rhythm of her words. "Sounds good."

It didn't. Being subjected to the inevitable viewing of HR videos and presentations would have him oscillating between boredom and panic over screwing something up. Neither was a pleasant prospect.

The elevator doors *whoosh*ed open, presenting him with the sight of a long corridor. A tall glass wall lined the far end from where they stood. Nancy pointed at the doors as she held the elevator open. "That's your new office. You'll find everything you need at the desk. Mr. Anderson will be in his office through to the right."

"Wait, you're not coming with me?" He was a grown man and didn't need to have his hand held, and yet the idea of facing the dragon on his own was terrifying. "But I thought we had a deal? We're married and stuff."

"That is probably why I'm still single. Plus, I have another meeting." Her gaze slid away from his. "I better get going or else I'm going to be late. I'll come by and check on you around noon, though, to make sure you don't need anything."

If he'd known her better, he would have totally called her on the obvious lie. "Probably just another cupcake. To keep my spirits up."

"I'll see what I can do." She smiled. "Good luck with everything."

"Thanks."

The elevator doors slid shut, leaving Nolan alone with nowhere to go but forward.

Well, then. Time to face the dragon.

His body didn't move.

God, not this again.

Deep breath. In and out.

You want this. You need this. Just because you have no idea what you're getting yourself into doesn't mean you can run away like a coward.

Sure. Okay. Not being a coward was now at the top of his mental training list.

Pulling back his shoulders, he got his feet going in the direction of the office.

The corridor wasn't all that long, and before he was mentally ready, he pulled the door open and stepped into his new domain. The desk had a sleek black top that would be chest-high for most people. Walking around the side revealed a nearly empty work area. A large flat-screen monitor took up a generous portion of the middle, flanked by a multiline phone. The chair looked to be expensive, and he couldn't resist taking a moment to sit down. Oh yeah, it was pretty damn comfortable. If the hours were going to be as long as Nancy thought they would be, at least his ass wouldn't get sore.

The lone file folder by the keyboard held a sheet of paper with his username and a temporary log-in password. Before he knew it, Nolan was in the system and setting up his email account. He scanned the appointments, made note of things he should read up on and others that looked to be irrelevant. His headache throbbed less as he lost himself in work. He'd need to get a pad of paper or something for his notes. Maybe they'd approve the purchase of a tablet if he was going to be out and around—

A loud cough made him jump. His gaze snapped to the man standing in the doorway of his office. Zack Anderson. Shit, he hadn't even noticed that the other man was there. "Sir?"

"What are you doing?" Mr. Anderson's voice was deep and sent a shiver through Nolan.

His new boss was every bit as intimidating *and* attractive as Nolan remembered. Mr. Anderson's dress pants were perfectly pressed, accentuating his thighs and hips. This morning he had on a light-blue dress shirt and a black tie that underscored the aura of confidence rolling off him. *Tina would laugh out loud if she knew I got a job* and *a hot boss.*

But like the first time they'd met, it was the intensity of his stare that was a punch to Nolan's chest. He felt as though Mr. Anderson could strip him bare with that look. He became aware of every imperfection that simmered beneath the surface of his clothes. Instinctively, his fingers found their way to his thigh to rub the ache. God, Anderson might be attractive to look at, but there was nothing about his personality that appealed to Nolan whatsoever.

It wasn't until Mr. Anderson cocked his eyebrow that Nolan realized he hadn't responded. Shit, he was really screwed if a single sentence did that to him. "I was reviewing your appointments for the day."

Mr. Anderson narrowed his gaze, and Nolan found himself jumping to his feet. *Time to earn your keep.* "You have a conference call in thirty minutes with Ms. Tan from the Singapore office of Raspberry. This is regarding the purchase of new monitors for the Vancouver satellite office. You then have a senior management meeting, followed by your monthly departmental update conference call. I was just making note of the files you would need and was going to ask if you had a preference for paper or electronic?"

Nolan's heart pounded in his chest, and he had to fight the urge to squirm as he waited for his boss to say something.

The seconds ticked loudly in his head, and he couldn't shake the feeling that he was being judged. *Jesus, help me.* His stomach flipped and churned as the tension pulled through him.

"Electronic." Mr. Anderson's voice remained stern, cold. "I take my coffee black, one sugar."

"Got it." No wonder people quit. In all his years as a trainer, he'd worked with a variety of individuals and no one had been as off-putting as Zack Anderson. "Is there anything else I can get for you before the meeting starts?"

The phone chose that moment to ring. Without hesitating, Nolan reached down and scooped up the handset, thankful for the distraction. "Good morning, Mr. Anderson's office. Hello, Mr. Chopra."

In that moment Nolan realized the dragon was human after all. The words were barely out of his mouth before his boss's eyes grew wide and he frantically shook his head. In a heartbeat he morphed from the indomitable *Mr. Anderson*, to simply *Zack* who really didn't want to talk to the man on the other end of the line. The ice melted, and in a rush of humor, the tension that had built up inside Nolan vanished.

"I'm very sorry, Mr. Chopra, he's in a meeting at the moment. No, no, I'm afraid I can't interrupt. Who am I? Nolan Carmichael, Mr. Anderson's new assistant. Yes, I do value my job. Again, I'm sorry that I can't interrupt him." The last time he'd run such heavy interference was when Tina's ex Malcolm had called, wanting to convince her to give him another shot. So far there was far less swearing with Mr. Chopra, but that was about the only difference. Nolan covered the mouthpiece with his hand. "I'll bring your coffee as soon as I'm done."

Zack didn't move immediately, which made dealing with the troublesome Mr. Chopra all the more challenging. Nolan's skin tingled where he knew Zack's gaze roamed. He wasn't getting a sexual vibe from his boss, more curiosity. As though Nolan was a puzzle that needed figuring out. Stupid, as he was the simplest man in the world. All he needed was to find a way to get on with his life, deal with his anxiety, and convince his sister that he really was a grown-up who could live on his own. If things were *really* going his way, he'd find a hot guy to climb into bed with on a semiregular basis for sweaty sex. Someone tall and strong, with brown eyes and hair.

A blush started to climb up his neck. *God, keep it in your pants.*

"Let me check his calendar to see when he might have an opening to meet with you."

As Nolan retook his seat, Zack spun on his heel and disappeared into his office.

"Are you even listening to me?" Mr. Chopra's voice rang in his ear.

"Yes, sir. Now it looks like Mr. Anderson is free a week from Thursday." Figuring out his boss would have to wait until later. Nolan had a job to do.

CHAPTER FOUR

Zack had finished his meetings for the day over an hour ago. Mondays were always long, filled with updates and check-ins from his global staff. It was an exhausting way to start his week, especially when he had to break in a new employee.

It had been frustrating to say the least. Not because Nolan had done anything wrong. If anything, his new assistant had been far more adept at handling tasks than Zack had assumed he would. The timidness Zack had witnessed in Nolan back in the bathroom was nowhere to be found. He'd dived into the meetings, emails, and reports that had been waiting for him. Zack had watched as Nolan would stare at something, shake his head, and plow through.

And yet.

Zack had been annoyed.

Every time Nolan tackled some task or other successfully, he'd smiled. Each time his lips curled up, something inside Zack had prickled. It wasn't even rational to be annoyed with someone for doing their job. To be rankled by another's success.

And yet.

This was proof that he was better off on his own. In the end, he would probably do Nolan a favor by letting him go. He'd save Nolan and himself a world of trouble; Nolan could find another job, and Zack could go back to doing what he wanted—being a prick.

For years, Zack had been the one who got things done. The heavy hand dragged in on a moment's notice to fix other people's screwups. At first it had annoyed him. He was a tech guy, never intended to be the corporate muscle. Then he took on purchasing for the department, then purchasing for all technology company-wide.

With each successive task that had landed on his plate, Zack had begrudgingly taken it on and eventually owned the hell out of it. His success rate grew, and with it came promotions. Three years ago he'd achieved the ultimate prize, the role of chief technology officer for Compass. Not bad for a computer guy with a business bachelor's and anger management issues.

Sure, he'd stepped on a few toes to get where he'd wanted to be, but those individuals had caused the company problems in the first place. He'd never once intentionally sabotaged someone's career to get ahead. He didn't need to. Patience was his virtue, and competence was his sword; he fixed everything and got Compass back on track.

It was dark outside, the only light coming from the harsh glow of the overhead fluorescents. His office door was open, and from his desk he had a clear vantage of Nolan's chair. It was empty, and he hadn't seen hide or hair of Nolan since before his last conference call. Annoyance prickled like fire ants beneath his skin. While his decision to hire Nolan might have been impulsive, the inevitable firing wouldn't be. It wasn't fair of him to place unrealistic expectations on his assistants, but he was who he was. If they couldn't handle it, then it was better for all involved to sever the relationship quickly rather than both of them suffer in protracted agony.

Nolan disappearing before Zack was done working on day one was a fast track to a pink slip.

Zack pushed to his feet, ignoring the muscle cramps racing through his back. The outer office was empty, but Nolan's computer was still turned on and the screen saver was flashing. A half-filled coffee mug held watch on the desk, flanked by the notebook Nolan seemed to have in his hand all day. Ridiculous for him to have a pen and paper method of keeping track of things, given he was the CTO's assistant. If Nolan survived through the first month, Zack would have to do something about that.

The key word was *if*.

First thing tomorrow he'd have to read Nolan the riot act about leaving without telling him. Or before Zack was done with him.

His back muscles protested again as he walked over to the small kitchenette around the side of the fake wall behind Nolan's area.

He'd been sitting far too much today and hadn't made it to Ringside last night to get some much needed work done on the place. Being there always helped him chill out and refill his emotional reserves. Given how much shit he still had to do before he called it a day, he'd have to miss another visit. At least he could do some stretching before he went back to work.

Coffee in hand, he returned to his office, kicked off his shoes, and flicked the light. He set his mug on his desk, pulled his tie free, and undid the top two buttons. That was better. His office was big enough that he didn't have to worry about moving any furniture out of the way.

Standing in the middle of the dark room, Zack closed his eyes and took a deep breath. Yoga had been one of the things Russel had forced him to learn as a teenager at Ringside. He'd wanted to move, run, hit things, not hold a tree pose with his eyes closed. He'd been surprised not only by how challenging it had been to learn the poses, but by how his mind and body had always felt clearer once he finished. Max and Eli hadn't kept up with the practice, but Zack had quickly made it a part of his routine, especially on days when the buzzing in his body didn't want to subside.

Taking another long breath through his nose, he bent his knees and stretched his arms out and above his head as he straightened into a mountain pose. Just as slowly he folded in on himself until his hands were flat on the floor. He groaned, enjoying the pleasant ache before going through the motions again. Over the years, yoga had helped him keep his temper in check. It was easy for him to slip into that mental place of peace with a few moves.

Zack was halfway through his routine when a noise from the outer office caught his attention. He froze on the spot when Nolan burst through the main doors, a stack of files in his arms and a headset flattening his hair.

"Yes, I understand that you need to speak with Mr. Anderson, but as I mentioned, Mr. Chopra, I can't get you an appointment any earlier than the one I've already booked."

Jesus, Raj needed to chill the hell out. Zack knew what the director wanted, and Raj knew his position on it—they'd been having the same argument for a month now—but he should also know Zack's mind wasn't going to be changed with a bombardment of annoying phone calls. Zack stepped toward his door, intending to say something to Nolan, when his assistant smiled.

"Yes, I understand your frustration. All I can do is promise you that I'll present the new information you've provided. Thank you for that email, by the way. Yes. Of course. No, I understand. But remember Mr. Anderson's approval is key to this. He's a reasonable man and will take all your information into consideration. Yes. I will. Have a good night, sir." Nolan ended the call and tossed the headset on his desk with a groan.

That had been . . . surprising.

Raj had driven his last assistant nearly insane with his constant calls. She'd begged Zack to deal with him, to talk to him, anything to get him to stop. As much as he pitied her, it was her job to manage those calls and difficult people. She hadn't seemed overly upset when he told her she was fired. At least Nolan had one thing going for him.

Two. He'd also stayed late.

Zack realized that Nolan didn't know he was still there, when he walked past the office with his mug over to the kitchenette. Zack heard splashing sounds—Nolan was washing the mug and, from the sound of it, the few other dishes in the sink. He shouldn't let Nolan do those, the cleaning staff would be around soon enough and that was part of their job, not his. Picking up his mug, Zack headed for the kitchenette and made a point of coughing before stepping past the threshold.

If Nolan was startled by his arrival, he didn't show it. "Hello, Mr. Anderson. How did your call go?"

There was something about the way Nolan said his name that irked him. "Call me Zack when we're alone."

Nolan paused briefly, then nodded. "No problem."

"I thought you'd left."

Nolan turned and looked at him wide-eyed. "Leave? I might have to live here for the next week to get caught up. Your appointment calendar is a mess, as are your files. I assume you've been the one handling these reports and approvals."

"I haven't had an assistant in eight months. Your predecessor lasted two days."

"Not surprising. The backlog alone would drive anyone to quit on sight." Nolan set the mugs in the drying rack and dried his hands off. "I've emailed you your agenda for tomorrow, along with the reports from the California office. You'll need those for your budget review next week. Also, I'm sure you just heard Mr. Chopra on the phone again. I understand your concerns with his proposal, but I reviewed the additional supporting documents he sent over today, and I believe he's addressed some of them. I wouldn't pass it along if I didn't think it was worth your time. That said, if you don't agree, I'll contact him once you've taken a look and break the news."

The man on the verge of a panic attack was nowhere to be seen. Nolan's shoulders were pulled back and his eyes sparkled with something Zack could only assume was excitement. That was, well . . . strange. No one ever enjoyed working for him, let alone this closely. Maybe there was something not quite right in Nolan's head.

Hands dry, Nolan lobbed his paper towel into the trash can. "I know it's only seven, but I was going to head home. Unless you need me for something else."

Zack moved closer, taking perverse pleasure in watching Nolan's hazel eyes widen with every step. He was shorter than Zack, but not by much. His wavy black hair was longer in front than Zack preferred on a professional, with a long forelock sort of like a pony's, but on Nolan it worked. It made him look handsome and vulnerable at the same time.

Where the hell did that come from?

Zack didn't look away and was impressed when, despite his obvious discomfort, Nolan didn't back down either. "What time do my meetings start tomorrow?"

Nolan swallowed, the tip of his tongue darting across his lips. "You originally had an eight o'clock with Finance, but I moved it to two, after your lunch meeting with Dell. I didn't see the sense in you needing to go out twice when one trip gets things sorted."

Okay, maybe he was going to have to keep Nolan around. Finance had refused his request for a meeting change twice. "I still expect you to be in by eight."

"If its fine with you, I'm going to keep the 7 a.m. start. It gives me time to get ready for the day and put out any fires before most people arrive. Plus it's quiet here at that time. It helps with my concentration."

Hard to argue with that logic, even if Zack suspected there was more to it than that. "Fine. I'll see you tomorrow."

Nolan nodded and turned to go, but stopped after only taking a few steps out of the kitchenette. "Are you okay, Mr. Anderson?"

"Zack." Why the hell did it matter what name Nolan called him by? Everyone referred to him by his surname.

"Sorry. Zack. You seem . . . off."

None of his assistants had ever stuck around long enough to care about how he felt, let alone noticed his emotional state on the first day. Given how little time they'd spent together interacting today, he couldn't imagine Nolan was that aware of his ebbs and flows yet. "It's been a long day."

"It has." Nolan hesitated a moment longer, before finally moving toward his chair. "Well, I'll see you tomorrow, *Zack*. Have a good evening."

Zack didn't move as Nolan gathered his things and left the office. He watched him stride all the way down the hall to the elevator and press the button. What was it about Nolan that had him paying such close attention? Yes, he was the first male assistant he'd had, but that shouldn't make much of a difference. He'd had closer working relationships with more men than he could count over the years. Things shouldn't be any different with Nolan. Even if he was attractive, intuitive, and made a perfect cup of coffee.

Nolan stepped into the elevator and stood sideways as he pressed the button. The doors slid shut without him meeting Zack's gaze. Maybe he wasn't as calm and collected about his new position as Zack assumed.

If Zack didn't want to be searching for his own files and yelling at Finance to change meetings again, then he'd have to take it a bit easy on Nolan. If nothing else, Nancy from HR would thank him for not scaring off someone else from the support team.

A wave of exhaustion hit him, and for the first time that day he wanted to leave the office and head home. Tomorrow he'd be fresh, and no doubt his abnormal kind streak would vanish and he'd return to his old habits. He gathered his things and did his best to ignore the lingering scent of Nolan's aftershave as he walked down the hall.

CHAPTER FIVE

That week, Nolan managed to average four hours of sleep per night. The early mornings didn't mean early evenings, and as Zack grew comfortable with him, he started asking him to do more and more. Now it was Friday, and for the first time since this whirlwind employment had begun, Nolan hoped that his boss would call it quits early. He wanted to go home and do nothing, shut his brain off while his body recovered.

Yeah, like that *was going to happen.*

When he wasn't actually working, he was home thinking about work. He was surprised on his third day of employment when Zack handed him a brand-new tablet. "It's embarrassing to see you using paper and pen." Nolan had been grateful and about to say something when Zack followed up with a quick, "But don't waste my time playing around setting it up."

So the last two evenings had been filled with him learning the new technology, operating system, and programs. Now, no matter the time of day, Nolan had access to Zack's schedule and Zack had unfettered access to him.

That was an oddly appealing thought.

The tablet was yet another mixed signal from his boss. The thoughtfulness of the tool so he could do his job more easily, versus the cold remarks he'd made when presenting it. This contradiction in Zack's personality had been digging at Nolan from the moment he'd laid eyes on him that first day. Nancy had warned him when he'd gone to chat with her in her office that once Zack got annoyed, Nolan would be on the receiving end of a barrage of negative remarks and picking. "He does try for a while, but he's just not a very nice person."

Her remarks had echoed in his ears the entire walk back to his desk.

The phone rang, jerking him from his thoughts. "Good afternoon, Mr. Anderson's office."

"Nolan."

A shiver rolled through his body at the sound of Zack's rumbling voice on the other end of the receiver. "Yes, sir?"

"Cancel my six o'clock with Jeremy. I ran into him earlier, and we discussed the shipping issues with Vancouver."

Three clicks and Jeremy was deleted into the ether. "Done. Anything else?"

"Go home."

Nolan frowned. "It's only four fifteen."

"I have a personal appointment that's going to take up my time, and I won't be back to the office. It's Friday. Go home."

Oh. That was more than a little unexpected. "Are you sure? I don't have any plans tonight and would be more than happy—"

"If you say another word, I'll fire your ass."

Nolan snapped his mouth shut. Zack was also quiet, and if it weren't for the hiss of the open line, he would have sworn his boss had hung up on him. The temptation to say something—ask a question, pretty much anything—was strong, but he had no doubt Zack really would fire him.

So he waited. Eventually, Zack cleared his throat. "This week was . . . positive. Given you've never done this job before, I didn't know what to expect. You surprised me."

"Thank you." He cringed and hoped the almost-compliment wasn't leading up to a death blow.

"Leave. I'll see you Monday." Zack hung up.

Nolan held the phone receiver out and stared at it for a few moments before replacing it on the hook.

Okay. That had happened.

He couldn't shake the feeling this was a test. Did Zack expect him to ignore the demand and stay, or did he genuinely want him to have an early weekend after putting in long hours all week? It shouldn't be this much of a problem, and he hated that his brain went off in search of problems when he should be gathering his things and leaving. Shit, he could get some takeout to bring home to Tina. They could celebrate that he was now gainfully employed and looking as though he might actually be able to keep the position. For the first time in a long while, Nolan smiled as he got to his feet.

If Zack were testing him, then there wasn't much he could do about it. He'd earned this. All week he'd managed to keep from having a panic attack as he'd focused on his new job while learning what it meant to be an executive assistant. That was a feat unto itself. Tonight he didn't have to be strong.

He ordered Chinese from their favorite take-out place and grabbed it on his way back to the apartment. By the time Tina got home from work, Nolan had the table set, the wine poured, and the music playing.

"Happy Friday!"

"You're home early." She dumped her things on the floor by the armchair and grabbed her glass of wine from him. "And I approve."

"Boss wasn't going to be coming back, so I got to leave. I wanted to give you a thank-you dinner." They clinked their glasses together. "To your neurotic brother finally becoming gainfully employed."

"Here, here." She swallowed down a large gulp. "Now all I need to do is get my neurotic brother back out to the clubs so he can find a hot guy to bang."

"No." Nolan turned his back on her and marched into the kitchen. "I'll get the food."

She strode just as quickly after him. "Come on. You haven't dated anyone seriously in years. You need to get back out into the world."

"I've been in rehab and not really dating material. Not to mention the whole freaking-out-in-large-crowds thing."

"So don't go somewhere that there's a large crowd." She took the bag that held the food containers out of his hand and put it back down on the counter. "I wasn't going to push you if the job didn't go well, but it did. For the first time since your accident I'm seeing the old you. You've been happy to leave the apartment every day. You're smiling, for God's sake. If your boss didn't sound like an asshole, I would tell you to go after him."

"I don't even think he's gay, so that wouldn't work."

She waved her hand. "Doesn't matter. What I'm saying is that you're finally on the mend. Honestly and truly getting better emotionally and spiritually. You need someone in your life, someone who will love you for the awesome person that you are."

It wasn't like Tina to hound him about this sort of thing. "What's going on?" Nolan put his wine down and gave her a hug. "Is everything okay?"

"Yeah." She hugged him back hard. "Really good. When I saw that you'd bought dinner and wine, I thought for a moment you'd heard my news."

Nolan pulled back, frowning. "News?"

She sighed. "Let's get this to the table and sit. It's good news. Mostly."

It was hard to wait even the few minutes it took them to relocate the food and wine to the table. His sister had been such a help to him over the past two years, had put a significant part of her life on hold for him, she deserved to have something positive happen. Nolan even went so far as to fill her plate with all of her favorites before he broke down. "Spill it."

"I don't want to ruin—"

"Tina."

"Okay, so I'm not sure if you remember the project I was on last year. The ad campaign for the new line of trucks?"

"I remember." There had been talk of her team winning some sort of advertising award. She'd been disappointed when it didn't happen.

"Well, it turns out that it wasn't just our department that had been impressed with what we'd done. I've been approached by senior management to lead a new department. It's a new position working mostly with a company in Japan, but it's a major contract and a huge promotion for me."

Nolan had always been a bit in awe of Tina's job and her work in advertising. The way she'd combined her skills in graphic design and psychology, and successfully moved up her company's ranks, had blown his mind. "Oh my God, sweetie. Congratulations! What's the problem?"

Her smile faltered. "That's because of the not-so-great news. If I accept the position, it means I have to move. The new team is at our Vancouver division."

As the words soaked into him, the panic he was sure she was worried about began to churn. "And you don't think your baby brother can handle life on his own? *Pfft.*"

"Please. I know you better than Mom and Dad. I know things have been hard on you. It broke my heart to see everything that you'd worked for taken away from you because of a fucking icy road."

"It was more the tree in the ditch that I hit than the road."

"Nolan!"

"Sorry." Leaning back, he ran his thumb along the rim of his plate. "I owe you so much, Tina. You saved my ass in more ways than I can count. A place to live, food, not teasing me when I was at my lowest. I know it's been hard on you, even if you haven't said anything."

As he spoke, Nolan knew there was only one thing he could do. Taking his glass in hand, he stood and held it out. "To my amazing sister. Let me be the first person to congratulate you on your promotion. I have no doubt that you're going to get that new team whipped into shape the same way you got me back to normal."

Tina's blush covered her face before Nolan finished speaking. "You're not normal."

"As close as I'm likely to get." He downed the remains of his glass. "When do you leave?"

"I told them I needed a weekend to think about accepting the position. I wasn't sure if I wanted to take it."

The fact that she'd been so worried about him, to the point where she was willing to turn down a promotion, annoyed Nolan. "You will."

"Then I'll have to give notice on this place."

Nolan looked around at the place that he'd called home for the past year. "I can take over the lease."

"What?"

"It makes sense. It's close enough to transit that I can get to the office without any problems. I've already got my stuff here. I should be able to afford it on my salary."

Tina's frown made her look like their mother. "What if you get fired? You said yourself that your boss was an asshole and not easy to get along with."

It was a risk, but it was Nolan's turn to step up and help his sister. "Nancy in HR told me that even if Zack cuts me loose, she'd find me a position somewhere else. You never know, maybe I'll get back into training again."

Tina's look told him all he needed to hear. No matter how much he might wish it, the chances of him getting back up in front of a room full of people would be slim to say the least. "That's something anyway."

"It's stability for me. Which means you don't need to worry about whether or not I'm going to fall apart, and you can call your boss and accept the promotion. You'll leave as soon as you need to, and I'll make sure everything is okay here." There. He said it with enough genuine excitement that he hoped she would listen to him.

One moment she was sitting beside him and the next she'd wrapped him up in a giant hug. "Thank you."

"For what?" He squeezed her tight.

"For understanding. For being one of the strongest people I know. For taking over my lease."

They both laughed. "Are you kidding? I'm too lazy to move my shit again. I was going to try and convince you to let me stay somehow."

"It's a one-bedroom."

"I would have totally shared a room with you. Because your couch is comfy and all, but lacking privacy."

"Yeah right."

Nolan lightly shoved her away. "Well, now I don't have to. I get the room all to myself."

"Now maybe you can find a guy and bring him back here for some sexy fun times."

He groaned. "Are we back to this?"

"Yes, yes, we are."

"I'm not going to have time to date, not with this job."

"You need to make time. I can't move to Vancouver if I think you're going to be here all alone. You're young and good-looking. There's a perfect man for you out there somewhere."

Sure, there was most likely the right man for Nolan out there, waiting for him to come along to sweep him off his feet. It wasn't as though he wanted to be perpetually single, but he'd gone from school to work, then smack into a life-altering accident. Finding someone to make out with hadn't been high on his priority list.

Nolan groaned. "I promise I'll do something. I'll try speed dating or sign up for a matchmaking site."

"Or." Tina's grin was not promising.

"Or?"

"We can go out tonight! Let's hit a bar, find some men, and have a good time."

"No."

"Come on. It'll be fun."

"It'll be hell." He shook his head, and Tina stuck her bottom lip out in a way he hadn't seen since they were kids. "Seriously?"

"How many more times are we going to have the chance to do this? Your job is going to take more and more time, and I could be moving in a few weeks." She took his hands in hers. "It's always been you and me, and we won't be like that much longer." She batted her eyes for good measure. "Come on. *Come ooonnn.*"

There was a reason the two of them had always gotten into trouble together as kids. Tina had an adventurous streak a mile wide, and Nolan couldn't say no to her.

"Okay. But I can't promise I won't have a panic attack and need to leave."

Tina whooped. "That's totally fine. You're getting out there and trying. That's all I can ask."

Apparently he was going out tonight. Nolan poured himself another full glass of wine and prayed things wouldn't end badly.

══ CHAPTER ══
SIX

Nolan's wine buzz had seeped through every inch of his body, so that by the time he and Tina fell out of the taxi and stumbled into line at Frantic, the last things on his mind were panic, anxiety, or even the pain that constantly lived in his leg. No, the only things he was aware of were the urge to giggle and the very nice ass of the man in front of him in line.

"Tina," he said in a voice that he hoped was a whisper. "Tina."

"What?"

He took her hand and gazed, wide-eyed and obvious, at the nice ass. "I need new jeans."

She giggled. "You're drunk."

"I think I might be." To prove the truth of the statement, he ignored Tina's protests and tapped the man on the shoulder. "Excuse me."

The man was shorter than Nolan, but far broader in the shoulders and chest. His brown eyes met Nolan's, and for a moment they reminded him of Zack's. *Jesus, this isn't any time to be thinking about your boss.* The man's lips curled into a soft smile. "Yeah?"

"I just wanted to let you know that you have a very nice ass."

The man's gaze raked down Nolan. He might be drunk, but he knew how he looked: tall, slight of build, his dress shirt a bit out of place at a club. When the other man's eyes returned to his, he shrugged and turned back around to continue talking to his friends.

Well, okay, then.

Tina pulled his arm. "Fuck him. You're hot and there will be lots of cute guys in there for you to flirt with."

Sure, there was that.

Frantic was his gay bar of choice, had been since he'd turned nineteen and was finally able to spread his wings and start clubbing. Well, start clubbing legally. Tina had always loved coming with him. The music was awesome, and she didn't have to worry about getting harassed by the guys. He hadn't been here since before his accident, and the normal anxiety he'd feel was currently being shoved aside by curiosity. The closer they got to the door, the louder the bass thumped and the greater his excitement grew. It had been ages since he'd given himself permission to let loose, to have fun and not worry about all the problems that had controlled his life for ages.

Tina skipped her way through the door ahead of him once they were finally waved through by the bouncer. Nolan didn't recognize him, but that wasn't surprising. No doubt there would be a great number of changes since his last visit.

The first was the sheer number of patrons crammed inside. Frantic had always been busy, especially on a Friday night, but the crowd of people on the dance floor was a claustrophobic sight.

Even his wine-soaked brain shouted a warning that this was A Bad Idea. He'd had many of those over the years, and really needed to learn to listen to that little voice.

Starting tonight.

"Tina, I think—"

"I love this song!"

Nolan stumbled forward as she jerked him out onto the dance floor and into the throng of people.

Okay, so this was happening. He was at a club with a shit-ton of people dancing to a cranked-up beat.

He had a choice: leave or dance. Bodies pressed against him, grinding to the rhythm of the song. He forced his feet to move and got to the outside edge of the dancers. Heat rolled off their bodies in waves as they writhed in front of him, silently encouraging him to join them. The wine buzz he'd been rocking made it difficult to get his brain working properly. His mouth grew dry and his breathing increased into shallow pants.

The acrid smell of sweat, the echo of voices around him, rattled his brain. A scream, a shout, an accidental shove that sent him stumbling startled him, and along with his balance he lost his hold on the present moment; memories flooded in while his guard was down. The cheers of the partiers morphed into the screams of Roberta, Simon, and Xi as his car spun out of control two years ago.

"Hey. Look out, you made me spill my drink . . ."

"Nolan! Look out!"

Somebody gasped, then all was quiet, the car silent as a ghost as it flew over the ice.

"Careful, buddy." A dancer pushed Nolan away. He hadn't realized that he'd moved.

The muscles in his chest tightened, and his vision started to go spotty. Air. He needed to get some fresh air, get away from people.

His leg throbbed, his head ached, a memory flashed through his mind of Roberta's body flying from the backseat of the car to smash into the windshield.

"Shit, Nolan! I think she's dead! Help us!"

Someone in the club puked, the smell unfortunately reinforcing his memories: Simon had panicked and fled the car, heaving his guts out as he went. Xi had helped Nolan with Roberta, who was severely injured but somehow, miraculously, had survived.

God, there'd been so much blood. Roberta's and his.

And the screams.

His vision darkened, and he lost his footing, swaying into a couple beside him.

"Sorry."

He needed to get out of here. Unable to focus properly on his surroundings, he pushed his way through the crowd and somehow found his way to the bar. "I need . . . ice water, please."

The bartender filled one and slid it over. "Are you okay?"

"No. Panic attack."

"Need me to get someone? Do you have a boyfriend here? A date?"

Nolan's fingers curled around the bar, helping to stabilize him. It should be easy enough to speak, to say no, to somehow squeak out Tina's name at the very least. But nothing could escape the tightening of his throat or the rising nausea.

When he heard the rumbling laughter that managed to cut through the chatter of voices and thumping bass, it didn't immediately register in his brain. Looking slowly over toward the sound, his body was shocked back to life when he saw Zack standing there. And he was smiling.

No, that couldn't be his boss. Not the man who, in the whole first week that Nolan had worked for him, had barely said a kind word. That man wouldn't be capable of grinning and carrying on with someone. Nolan blinked quickly, trying to clear the obvious mirage from his eyes. Nope, Zack was still there.

"Buddy?" The bartender patted his hand. "Dude, are you going to pass out on me?"

Nolan sucked in a deep breath and managed to tear his gaze from his couldn't-possibly-be boss. "I'm . . . Washroom?"

"Down the hall to the left."

He pushed away from the bar and followed the directions, staring at his feet to avoid being overwhelmed by the lights, colors, and flailing bodies. He needed distance from the crowds, find a quiet place to catch his breath and then get his head straight. *Yeah right.* It would be fine. *No it won't.* He'd get himself under control enough that he could get the bartender or one of the bouncers to find Tina. *You're fucking broken.* Barring that, he'd take a cab home and apologize to Tina when she got home. *Dead on the side of the road.*

The line to get into the bathroom was bordering on impressive and rivaled the line to get into the club in the first place. *Too many people.* He closed his eyes. Shit, this wasn't going to work.

His chest tightened as a cold sweat rolled across his body. He blindly felt for the wall, but missed and found nothing but empty air. Really he should open his eyes, but the lights were causing his head to throb on top of everything else. He tried again, this time coming in contact with a warm body. "Sorry."

"Nolan?" God, he was really far gone if he was conjuring up such a realistic version of Zack's voice. "It *is* you. The bartender asked me to come after you. Said you looked like you recognized me."

Help me.

Don't look at me.

Save me.

He wanted to say something, but it was getting harder for him to breathe. All he managed was to force his eyes open a crack, just enough to confirm that yes, it really was his boss who was witnessing his freak-out.

Wonderful.

Zack was talking to someone else, but Nolan couldn't register who that was. No doubt a date who'd had their evening ruined by Nolan's panic.

A strong arm slipped around his waist and started to move him. "Come with me."

He didn't have much of a choice, given how badly he needed Zack's physical support. With each step they took, the sounds lessened and Nolan was able to hear himself think again. Zack pushed a door open and maneuvered him to a leather chair. "Put your head down between your knees. Try and breathe in through your nose and out through your mouth."

Zack's voice was steady, unemotional, the exact thing Nolan needed. So was the large hand pressed against the back of his neck: it wasn't a gentle caress or even a friendly pat. Zack's grip was firm, grounding, a focal point that Nolan could mentally grab hold of and use as a center. The air shuddered and forced its way through his nasal passage, and came rushing out through his mouth. He had to concentrate hard to slow it down, to get a handle on that simple, life-giving task so he wouldn't faint on his boss's shoes.

After some time had passed—he had no idea how much—he was eventually able to sit up. It was only then that Zack moved his hand away and set a respectable distance between them.

"Are you okay?"

Nolan had to swallow twice before his voice worked. "No."

"Are you here with someone?" There was a strange tone in Zack's voice. "Were you here on a date?"

"Came with my sister. She wanted to celebrate a promotion."

Zack nodded. "Her name?"

"Tina Carmichael."

"I'll have Max make an announcement on the PA and get her in here."

"Thanks."

Zack sat down on the edge of the desk behind him. "What happened?"

"I get these . . . anxiety attacks. I was in an accident a few years ago, and I've had them ever since."

"The crowd got to you?" Zack cocked his head to the side. "That's why you're not in training any longer."

"I don't want to talk about it."

"Fine."

Silence fell between them, and Nolan used the time to run through some of the mental exercises his counselor had drilled into him. It was only after he'd gone through two of them that he realized Zack was staring at him. "What?"

"You're gay."

"Yes. So are you apparently."

A muscle jumped in Zack's jaw. "Is that a problem?"

Nolan shook his head. "Why the hell would you being gay be a problem for me?"

"I'm your boss."

"Are you about to demand sexual favors from me?"

"No."

"Then it's not a problem." And because they were apparently having this conversation despite how shitty he was feeling: "I have no intention of outing you, if that's your concern. I don't discuss my colleagues' personal lives or engage in office gossip." Well, not with anyone at work. Tina would no doubt grill him when she found out.

"I'm not in the closet." Despite his assurances, Zack didn't look at all comfortable. "I'll go ask Max to find your sister. Will you be okay on your own for a minute?"

Nolan nodded and closed his eyes. He needed a few moments alone to let his brain catch up to everything that had happened in such a short period of time.

Zack was gay. His very good-looking albeit abrupt boss was gay. Zack wasn't exactly his type, but knowing himself the way he did, he'd end up reading more into everything Zack did from this point on.

Not to mention Zack now knew the ugly truth about his anxiety.

He was hit by the scent of Zack's cologne when he came back into the office.

"Max is going to make the announcement and will bring her back."

"Thanks." Even with his eyes closed, Nolan was aware of Zack moving around the room. "You're pacing."

"Just thinking."

Of course it was now time for the inevitable barrage of questions. "Go ahead."

"What?"

"Ask me whatever you need to. It's fine."

The pause stretched on. "What happened?"

Nolan was cut off as Tina rushed through the door. "Nolan!" She was accompanied by the man he'd seen speaking to Zack at the bar. No doubt the mysterious Max. "Oh my God, are you okay? I should never have made you come out."

"I'm fine. Need to get home."

Tina brushed hair from his face. "I'll get a cab."

"I'll drive you home." Zack pushed from the desk.

Tina frowned and looked between them. "And you are?"

"I'm Zack Anderson. Nolan's boss."

Her eyes widened briefly, but that was the only indicator of her surprise. "I don't want to interrupt your evening."

"I was here for business." Zack gave Max's shoulder a squeeze. "I'll give you a call next week, and we can work out the details."

"Sounds good."

Tina helped Nolan to his feet. "Let's get you outside."

Max opened the office door. "There's an employee entrance here. It's close to Zack's car, and you won't have to go back into the crowd. This way."

It was strange, given all the external stimuli that hit Nolan the moment they left the office, but the one thing he was acutely aware of was the warmth of Zack walking behind him.

The fresh outside air helped ease his tension. Tina's unwavering presence helped as well.

Zack moved past them and to a black Audi SUV. "Let me shift some papers from the backseat."

Tina took that distraction as an opportunity to tug Nolan closer. "Your boss?"

"Yup."

"He's gay."

"Yes, I've just discovered that."

"He's hot."

"Please, I'm begging you. Don't do this. I'm barely able to walk, much less think with my dick."

When Zack pulled back, papers in hand, he left the door wide open. "Here you go."

Blood and screams and vomit.

Tina tugged at Nolan. "Let's get you home."

He'd have to get into the vehicle to make that happen. He'd have to put his trust in someone else behind the wheel because he was never *ever* driving again.

"Nolan?" Tina's voice shook. "Are you okay?"

"Yup." He took a breath and let her guide him into the backseat. Zack shut the door as soon as Tina slid in beside him, then quickly jumped into the driver's seat.

"Address?" Zack threw the car into reverse without putting his seat belt on. "I'll pop it into the GPS."

"Seat belt." The word came out clear, but too soft for Zack to hear.

"It's 25 Wellesley Street East," Tina said as she clicked her seat belt into place.

Zack started to pull out of the parking lot. "Okay, won't take long."

"Put your seat belt on!" Nolan's body shook and sweat broke out across his skin. "Put it on now!"

Zack stopped the car and stared at him wide-eyed in the rearview mirror. "Right. Sorry."

It wasn't until Nolan heard the telltale click that he was able to relax and close his eyes.

Tina had been through enough of these incidents to know not to talk to him much on the drive home. He caught Zack staring at him at every red light they hit.

The silence lasted until Zack pulled up in front of their apartment. "Do you need any help?"

"I've got him." Tina collected their things and jumped out.

Zack never took his eyes from Nolan. "Are you sure?"

He wasn't sure about anything—not himself, not his life, and certainly not his hard-ass boss. "I'll be fine. Thank you."

Zack didn't drive away until they stepped into the entranceway of the building. Tina paused long enough to watch him go. "I totally get it now."

"Get what?"

"Never mind. Let's put you to bed."

He'd have to ask her another time what she'd meant by that. Right now, he couldn't focus on anything but going to sleep. Everything else he'd deal with tomorrow.

= CHAPTER =
SEVEN

The boardroom emptied quickly at the conclusion of Zack's Monday morning department meeting. He'd been a bit sharper than normal, and doubtless no one wanted to wait around long enough to get stuck in a one-on-one situation with him. His foul mood wasn't caused by anyone in the meeting, nor any of the myriad reports that had flowed near-seamlessly together. It wasn't even his unexpected run-in with Nolan on Friday night at the club. He'd been worried about his assistant over the weekend, but knew Nolan was in his sister's apparently more than capable hands.

He'd been in a perfectly fine mood until Max had emailed him first thing this morning.

I'm sorry dude, but the investor backed out. Back to square one.

Fuck, after everything they'd done, to see it all get pissed down the drain because some idiot venture capitalist got cold feet? *That* ticked him off.

When he'd eventually made it into the office, Nolan wasn't anywhere to be seen. There were signs that he was around—a fresh mug of coffee on his desk, a new stack of papers beside the phone—but the man himself was away. Probably for the best. As much as Zack wanted to make sure he was okay, it wasn't fair to inflict his current mood on him.

He'd spent a few hours searching on the internet Saturday morning, trying to learn as much as he could about the accident Nolan had mentioned. There hadn't been much. A small online article describing the events. Single vehicle accident due to bad road conditions. Nolan and three passengers had been in the car when the accident occurred. Nolan and a woman had been air lifted to the hospital in Toronto. There wasn't anything else he could find, which meant he'd have to ask the man involved if he wanted to further sate his curiosity.

"Mr. Anderson, you're all alone."

He looked up to see Samantha Rollins's slim frame in the doorway. "Do you have the room?"

"I do, but there's no rush. You okay? You were a million miles away."

He'd learned long ago not to even attempt lying to his boss. Not that he would, at any rate; the truth was far easier to keep track of. "Pondering my new assistant."

"I heard you took another kick at that particular can. Going to fire him too?"

He snorted. "No. Not yet at least."

"That's good. Your reputation as a boss is crap. I might have to make it a line item in the company employee satisfaction evaluation."

"Is it that time of year again?" He groaned when she nodded. "Have fun sucking up. I'll accept my poor grade with pride."

"I'm as likely to have a poor evaluation as you are." She came fully into the room. "Though I'm glad you have another assistant. You've needed the help for a long time now."

"I'm good on my own."

"So you say, but everyone needs help. Especially stubborn-ass men like you."

Zack got to his feet and collected his things. "Nolan is just as stubborn. I found out this weekend that he can't do crowds. Panic attacks, kind of a posttraumatic stress thing from a bad accident a few years ago."

"That's horrible. He's okay though? I mean, he can handle working here?"

Samantha might look like a sweet, innocent woman, but Zack had seen her cutthroat side far too many times to buy her concerned tone. "He'll be fine."

"Well, you have three months to let him go without cause. Just make sure you don't screw up and miss the deadline."

"I'll keep that in mind. I have another meeting in fifteen. I'll see you tomorrow."

"Take care."

It wasn't fair to put Nolan under the light that way, but the alternative was worse. If Samantha got wind of his side project with Max, Zack's position at Compass would become far less stable. His end goal was to get the hell out of here, but not before he was ready. With the timetable now up in the air, it was even more important for him to keep his nose clean.

When he stepped out of the conference room and turned the corner to go down the corridor that led to his office, he was suddenly faced with the sight of Nolan standing in front of the office door, blocking it from an angry woman. He didn't need to come too close before he was able to hear that Nolan's normally patient tone was strained.

"I'm sorry, ma'am, but as I said, I'm not able to let you in."

"You have no right! Get out of my way." The woman hit Nolan's arm.

"What's going on here?" Zack's voice bounced down the hallway.

The woman spun on her heel to face him as Nolan slumped against the door. "You asshole!"

He looked at her hard, but he didn't recognize her. "Why are you assaulting my assistant?"

"You don't even know who I am?" She growled and marched closer. "Of course you don't. Why the hell would you remember me when you didn't pay my sister the time of day and she worked for you?"

Zack stopped as she got within a foot. He didn't know her, but there was something familiar about her face. The fullness of her cheeks and the shade of her blue eyes. The realization hit him. "You're Miranda's sister."

"Well good for you. I'm surprised you even knew her name."

Miranda had been his second-to-last attempt at working with someone before Nolan. She'd been fantastic at first, organized and efficient in a way that would have put Nolan to shame. When she turned out to be moody and short-tempered at times, a few people around the office complained, but Zack ignored it; he didn't feel he could fault her for traits he exhibited to an even greater extreme.

And she got the job done. Everything had been going fine until he caught her sneaking a corporate laptop out one night. She'd claimed she was only using it for the night, and he'd let it go. But then other things around the office had gone missing, and he'd been left with no choice but to confront her. When she'd admitted to stealing a number of company items, and to having a history of kleptomania, he'd fired her but not pressed charges.

Zack had also suggested she seek help, and she'd said she was already in treatment; she hadn't sounded very optimistic about that, however. Mostly she'd seemed mortified and defeated. It turned out that the missing items were all in the trunk of her car, in a reusable shopping bag; she'd handed it to the security guard who'd ushered her out.

Nolan had disappeared into the office and quickly picked up the phone. No doubt he was calling security to have the irate woman removed from the building.

Zack only needed to stall long enough for them to arrive. "What can I do for you?"

"You can do nothing for me. I just wanted to give you this." She reached into her purse, yanked out an envelope, and shoved it to his chest. "Here."

He took it from her but didn't open it. "What's this?"

Her lip quivered. "Miranda . . . passed away a few weeks ago."

Miranda's troubles had run deep. From her sister's anger, and the way she said the words, Zack couldn't help but think Miranda's passing hadn't been from natural causes. "I'm sorry for your loss."

"Sure you are." She cleared her throat. "We had the reading of her will this week. She'd asked me to deliver this letter to you. Now that I have, I'm done with you. You can tell your lapdog I'm leaving. He won't have to wait for security." She pushed past him and marched to the elevator.

When Zack was finally able to move again, he walked back into his office and quietly sat behind his desk. Nolan followed him.

"Mr. Anderson . . . Zack, I'm so sorry about that. She caught me as I was coming back from the mailroom, and was demanding to see you. I don't have a clue how she got past security." Nolan snapped his mouth shut as he stood in front of the desk. When Zack finally looked up, he saw that Nolan was frowning. "Are you okay?"

"She was the sister of a previous assistant."

"Oh."

"Miranda is dead. I think she might have killed herself."

Nolan's eyes widened. "Shit."

Zack held the letter up for Nolan to see. "This is from her."

"You fired her?"

It would be easy to tell Nolan his reasons, to show that his actions were justifiable. He'd made a decision back then, when he didn't pursue charges against her, that he would keep her transgressions between them. Now that she was dead, there was no point tarnishing her name. "I did." He couldn't look at the letter, didn't even want to hold it any longer. He opened his drawer and shoved the envelope into the middle of the stack of papers. "We should probably talk about this weekend."

Nolan had proved capable at the day-to-day tasks his job required, but if the anxiety was going to be a concern, Zack needed to know sooner rather than later. He might like Nolan, but he couldn't risk running into another problem like Miranda: an otherwise competent assistant with an insurmountable flaw.

For his part, Nolan looked far from comfortable. "Yes, we probably should."

"I hired you rather impulsively. You were overqualified, and I liked your honesty the first time we spoke. So I need to know if what I saw happen at the club is going to be a problem here."

Zack watched as an array of emotions raced across Nolan's face. What he didn't expect was for Nolan to lean forward, hands braced on the desk, and lock gazes with him. "I was glad for your help, but I'd have managed without it. I was starting the techniques I've learned to calm myself down, and in another few minutes I would have pulled myself together enough to find my sister or call a cab. I wouldn't have been great, but I'd have gotten home. And the fact that I could go out at all is the result of two years of hard work. There was a time I could barely leave my house; I've come a long way since then. I'm not one hundred percent, but I'm everything I need to be to do this job. If you want to fire me after what you saw, do me the courtesy of letting me go now before I've invested too much time here."

The unspoken *before I've invested too much time in you* came across loud and clear. Nolan wasn't Miranda, and as tempting as it was, Zack had no right to pass judgment on him for something that had been outside of his control. "When's my next appointment?"

Nolan stood and straightened his tie. The fire that had sparked in his eyes faded. "Not for two hours. Would you like a coffee?"

"I'm good."

As Nolan left him to take his chair at his desk, Zack realized he was not just good; he was great. Despite what had happened Friday night, having Nolan around had been helpful in more ways than he could count. What Nolan did outside of work was none of Zack's concern. Nolan had proven himself more than any of his other assistants in a shorter period of time. The two of them fit professionally, which was a new experience for Zack.

His gaze drifted to the closed drawer that held Miranda's letter. He should read it.

Maybe later.

It was hard, but he tried to bring up something positive about her. She hadn't been a happy woman, even back then. After her first few days on the job, Miranda had rarely smiled, and her moods had been volatile. Looking back, the signs of depression were clear. If he'd only paid a bit more attention to her, he might have found the opportunity to do something, to have helped her. Changed the course of events that led to her dying far too young.

The phone in the outer office rang. "Good morning, Mr. Anderson's office."

It might be too late for him to do anything for Miranda, but it wasn't too late for Nolan. Zack didn't need to insert himself into Nolan's life to help him. He could just keep providing what he already did: a stable job and the opportunity for Nolan to move through the organization when he was ready. Nolan was smart, talented, and could clearly handle himself. Hell, if he could stand up to Zack's grouchiness, then he'd make a name for himself soon enough.

Nolan laughed, and the sound of his rich voice made Zack's cock stiffen.

There were many things Zack could do for Nolan, but dragging him into a flirtation wasn't one of them. Pushing down on his hard cock, he turned to his computer, determined to forget about troublesome assistants and get to work.

═ CHAPTER ═ EIGHT

Nolan was neck-deep into reviewing a department budget when the office door opened. Nancy stood there, grinning like a fool, her hands behind her back.

"Good morning!" She stepped in close and placed a plate with a very large and decadent cupcake on his desk. "Congratulations."

Without missing a beat, he swiped his finger through the icing. "Buttercream. Damn, that's good."

"It better be. I had them special make it. Black forest cheesecake base and cherries inside."

Nolan forgot all about the report and dove into his treat. "What is this for? My birthday isn't even close."

Leaning forward so she could peek into Zack's office, Nancy relaxed when she saw he wasn't there. "You are the first assistant to Mr. Anderson who's made it past the three-week milestone."

It was absolutely mental that there was even a need to mark such a milestone. Not that he had any intention of giving back his cupcake. "Was there any doubt?"

"I probably shouldn't tell you this, but there was a betting pool in HR as to how long you'd last."

Nolan's face heated. "How long did you give me?"

"Oh, I won the bet three days ago. No one thought you'd survive to this point. I have to say, I'm really happy you did. Complaints about Mr. Anderson have dropped by eleven percent. In three weeks. That's huge!"

"How many complaints have there been about me?"

She grinned. "You're up to three now, but they're all serial bitchers, so it's fine."

It was hard to believe he'd been at Compass that short of a time. It certainly felt far longer, given how much he'd accomplished. He had fallen into a routine, one that gave him a sense of peace. Up early every morning, he would do his physiotherapy exercises before scarfing his breakfast and getting a coffee to go. He worked late more often than not, spending the last hour of each day with Zack in his office, reviewing reports and the next day's schedule. Tina had complained that he'd become a very messy ghost inhabiting her apartment; she never saw him anymore.

Sure, he probably didn't need to spend quite so much time at work. He might have eased up a bit if it weren't for the fact that, although Tina had accepted her promotion, she'd put off the move. Despite her protests to the contrary, it was obvious she didn't believe he would be able to handle living on his own. Her company would only let her stay in Toronto for so long before demanding that she relocate, and the last thing Nolan wanted was to be the reason for a big opportunity to fall through on her.

Nolan loved his family, especially his sister, more than anything. The two of them had always been close, and sharing an apartment had only brought them closer. But it was too easy to rely on someone all the time, to know that if things got even a bit challenging for him, he had a safety net in the form of his sister. He'd been grateful for Tina's help after the accident—he couldn't have made it without her support—but he wasn't a child or an invalid. They'd reached a fork in the road and, for the first time since they were kids, they had to each take a different path.

Tina needed to move on.

So did he.

Nancy jerked him from his thoughts when she reached over and took her own swipe of frosting. "Damn, that is good. I'm going to have to go back and get some for myself."

"I might go too. My sister would love these." Over Nancy's shoulder, Nolan saw the elevator doors slide open. Zack emerged, chin lowered as he strode down the hall toward the office like a man possessed. "Oh no."

Nancy straightened. "He's coming, isn't he?"

"And looking pissed."

"Well it was nice knowing—"

Zack pushed the door open. "Nolan! My office."

"Yes, sir."

Nancy grimaced. "Well, I'll let you get to it." Without looking once at Zack, she scampered away.

Coward. "Do I need anything specific?"

Zack threw . . . something . . . his tie? And his blazer? "Asshole!"

Shit.

The muscles in Nolan's chest started to tighten, making it difficult to take long, deep breaths. Still, he had a job to do. Ignoring the rising anxiety, he grabbed his tablet and entered the lion's den.

Zack's hair was sticking up in a very unnatural way. Nolan knew it would be the wrong move to run his hand through it, to smooth it down so Zack looked more like his normal, put-together self. Instead, he walked over to where Zack's tie and blazer lay in a heap on the floor. The material was still warm from Zack's body, and Nolan held it to his chest. "What can I help with?"

"I need to write an email. I'm fucking pissed."

"I got that."

Zack glared. "Don't push."

"Sorry." Nolan coughed as he placed Zack's clothing on the guest chair. "What do you need me to do?"

"You're going to type. I'm going to dictate. Because if I write this myself, I'm going to get fucking fired."

There was something about the tone of Zack's voice that tightened Nolan's chest even more. "Sure. At whom are we screaming?"

"Chopra."

Nolan wanted to groan but managed to stop himself. Instead he moved around Zack's desk and sat down in the chair. "I need you to unlock your computer."

Zack came around behind him and leaned over his shoulder. "I need to give you my password so you can do this shit yourself."

"I'm fairly certain the CTO has a policy against that." Nolan forced his head straight, doing his best to keep some distance between them. "Thank you."

When Zack finally pulled back, Nolan took a deep breath and mentally counted backward from ten. He cleared his throat again. "Email open. Let's start."

Zack started pacing. "Dear asshole."

"Dear Mr. Chopra."

"I *told* you the deal. What the fuck did you think would happen when you went over my head?"

"It was unfortunate how our last meeting progressed."

"Did you think I wouldn't find out? That Samantha dislikes me so much she'd ignore my concerns?"

"I've met with Ms. Rollins and we've reviewed your proposal. At this time, she shares my concerns regarding your plan."

Zack stopped pacing and turned to face him. "You think this is a joke? This is your fault. You encouraged him. You let him think I was going to take this shit seriously. He's trying to get his brother-in-law's company in as an exclusive supplier, one that I'm fairly certain he'd be receiving kickbacks on. I'd pretty much shut him down until you gave him hope."

Nolan's hands hovered over the keyboard. He tried to remain calm and keep his mind focused as Zack lit into him. Sure, he wasn't a business expert, but the documents that Mr. Chopra had forwarded to Nolan seemed legitimate enough. How was he to know there was a family member involved? Or that Chopra would go over Zack's head? "I'm sorry. I didn't—"

"Of course you didn't know! Christ. You're not even a real fucking assistant. I don't know why I hired you."

With each word that Zack spat, Nolan's heartbeat increased. It pounded in his ears, drowning out the words. Not that he needed to hear them. All he needed to know was the look of unfiltered anger on Zack's face. The way his eyes flashed, the red hue of his skin, the throbbing of blood pulsing beneath the surface of his skin.

He looked the same way Roberta's husband had when he'd stormed into Nolan's hospital room after the accident.

This is your fucking fault! She'll never walk again!

"Sorry," he managed to squeak out again.

Zack said something else, but Nolan could no longer make out the words. The pounding in his head was deafening as he fought to pull air into his lungs.

Time stopping as the car slid across the ice.

Screams and blood and pain.

A flash of lights as he tried to open his eyes, a glimpse of faces in medical masks.

Roberta silent, Xi panicked.

Metal from the door jammed into Nolan's leg.

"Your fault . . . your fucking fault . . ."

Impact.

His vision blurred, and for a moment he thought the world was going to bottom out. He was only vaguely aware of a touch on his shoulder and the office chair being moved. Hands at his throat, not choking, but pressing down toward his shoulders, removing the tightness.

"Breathe."

Nolan complied, gasping and praying that the air would make it to its destination.

"Again. Breathe."

He closed his eyes and did as he was told. With no concept of time, he focused on the little things. The weight of Zack's hands on his shoulders. The commanding tone of Zack's voice as he continued to tell Nolan what to do, guiding him through the blindness of his panic.

Finally, Nolan's sight returned, and he blinked rapidly when he realized that Zack's face was off to the side mere inches from his. "I'm fine."

"Bullshit. You're pale and sweating."

"That'll go away." He tried to stand, but Zack held him still.

"I'll get you some water. Just stay there."

He missed Zack's warmth as he stood and moved back, but appreciated the space. "Thank you."

The screen saver danced on Zack's monitor. Streaks of light zipped across the blackness, helping Nolan focus on something other than his embarrassment. Now, not only would Zack be angry at him, he'd realize that the anxiety was far worse than not being able to handle a crowd. That when he'd asked for honesty, Nolan hadn't given him a realistic picture. How could Nolan hope to give Tina the peace of mind to move if he couldn't handle a stern piece of criticism from his boss?

Assuming Zack didn't fire his ass.

Zack marched back into the office, holding Nolan's coffee mug. "Drink this." He held it out for him, but kept his distance.

The water held a hint of coffee as he swallowed it down. Thankfully, it helped, and finally he knew things had settled. Zack continued standing, his gaze locked on him, and Nolan felt compelled to respond. "I'm not going to die on you. Don't worry."

"I am. Worried."

"Don't be. And don't feel as though you can't fire me. If I screwed up, and it sounds like I did, then you need to let me go."

"We can discuss your screw up later."

"No." Nolan got to his feet, stumbling briefly before his muscles decided to cooperate. "I can't work like that. You're a control freak with some of the biggest anger issues I've ever seen. You yell at the world and expect it to do your bidding. I've done my best to work with you, and up until a short time ago, I thought I'd been doing a pretty good job." The anger helped, gave his surplus of adrenaline a new focus. The surge pushed Nolan past his anxiety, giving him a temporary burst of energy.

Zack continued to stand still. His lips were parted, moist where he'd licked them. His eyes fixed on Nolan as he moved closer.

"Did you know that HR had a bet going about how long I'd last? They didn't even give me three weeks. I might not have experience as an assistant, but that bet had nothing to do with my abilities and everything to do with you being an asshole. You'd heard me dealing with Mr. Chopra, and if you didn't like the way I handled him, or expected me to know things about that situation that weren't in the file, you had every opportunity to tell me. But you didn't. There's apparently no pleasing you, and in the long run you were bound to find some reason I wasn't cutting it, no matter how hard I worked or how well I did. So if you're going to fire me, do it now, so I can get on with my life."

Nolan had moved within inches of Zack. Their faces were so close that their breaths mixed between them. Nolan's anger might have given him fuel for a brief time, but he knew it wouldn't be long before exhaustion took over. He wanted this handled before that happened, so he could leave with his head held high.

"I'm not going to fire you."

His body relaxed. "I'm sorry if I made things difficult for you with Ms. Rollins. I'll even send the email to Mr. Chopra so you don't need to deal with him."

Zack reached out and cupped Nolan's elbow. "Tomorrow."

"I can get it done—"

"Tomorrow. I'll drive you home."

"That's not necessary—"

Zack placed his other hand on Nolan's other arm. "I just sent you into a full-blown panic attack because I lost my head. I *was* an asshole. The least I can do is see that you make it home safe."

Oh, it was so tempting to take him up on that. To let himself be taken care of once again, to not have to worry about going it alone. Tempting, but not something he should be doing. "I'll call a cab."

The muscle in Zack's jaw jumped. "You're stubborn."

"No worse than you."

"You're not well." Zack tightened his grip on Nolan's shoulder.

"Well enough to get home." He licked his lips as his gaze drifted to Zack's mouth.

When it came, the kiss was explosive. Nolan's eyes slammed shut at the press of Zack's mouth against his. Hot tongue invaded, dancing with Nolan's as their chests pressed against one another. His head spun and his body shook at the abrupt change of mood; his emotions bounced from anger to desire to confusion. What the hell was going on?

As abruptly as the kiss began, Zack pulled back. "Damn it." He looked at Nolan, eyes wide and clearly shocked. "I'm sorry. I shouldn't have done that."

"It's fine."

"No. It really isn't." Zack moved, snatching his blazer and tie from where Nolan had set them down. "You're fine to get home alone?"

Don't go! "I'm good."

Zack nodded, hesitating only for a moment before leaving. "I'll see you tomorrow."

Nolan stood alone in the office, shaken and confused. What the hell had happened? What was it about Zack that threw him into utter turmoil? He knew that despite what he'd said, there was no way he'd be able to get himself home. He pulled his phone from his pocket, and dialed Tina.

"Hey. I need you to come get me."

"Are you okay? You don't sound good."

Not even a little. "Just come get me."

═ CHAPTER ═
NINE

Zack carried the taste of Nolan on his lips all the way to the car. The scent of him had taken up residence in Zack's brain and there was nothing he could do to free himself. Going home to his condo would leave him with his thoughts and feelings. Given what had just happened, that was not a good thing. He needed to lose himself, to distance himself from his actions.

What he needed was a drink.

It didn't take long for him to detour to Frantic. While the idea of going to a dance club wasn't at the top of his list of things he wanted to do at three in the afternoon, Max would be there. If nothing else, he'd be able to hide in Max's office with a bottle from the top shelf and not have to worry about sitting at a bar drinking alone.

The cleaning staff were just arriving at Frantic, and Zack followed them inside, earning him more than a few odd looks. House music echoed uncomfortably in the empty space that would normally be filled with half-naked bodies. He could picture Nolan here, dancing along with the crowd. The way his too long hair would fly around his face as his hips swayed to the heavy beat. The red flush that would cover his cheeks.

The same flush Nolan had when the anxiety took him over today.

Zack cursed as he walked past the bar and made his way to Max's office. His friend was typing something at his computer when Zack barged in unannounced. "I need a drink."

Max raised an eyebrow and pushed away from his desk. "Hello to you too."

"I'm an asshole."

"And have been as long as I've known you. Any specific reason for your revelation this afternoon?"

He fell into the chair opposite Max and waited for the emergence of the Scotch and two glasses that he knew were in the bottom drawer. "I sent my assistant into a full-blown anxiety attack."

"Worse than the one he had here a few weeks ago?"

"I thought I was going to have to take him to the hospital."

"Jesus." Max filled Zack's glass to the point where if he drank it all he knew he wouldn't be driving himself anywhere. "Is he okay? Did you get him home?"

"He wouldn't let me." The Scotch burned as he drank it down. Zack knew the sting wasn't much of a punishment for what he'd done, but it was all he could manage.

"Can't say that I blame him." Max leaned back in his chair. "What did you do?"

"I lost my temper."

"Was it his fault?"

"Yes. No. Not really."

"Then unless you're going to fire him, you better make sure you have an awesome apology waiting for him tomorrow."

Zack took another drink. "Yeah."

"What aren't you telling me? Because no matter how cute assistant boy is—and he's quite the hot number—if he was even a little incompetent you wouldn't hesitate to let him go. So the fact that you're sitting here drinking a very nice Scotch without so much as tasting it means that this is more than you losing your temper."

Max was the one person who knew Zack, almost better than he knew himself. There was no point in lying, because sooner or later he'd figure out the truth.

"I kissed him."

"Idiot." Max took another drink before topping up both their glasses. "Did he freak out?"

"Don't know. I didn't stick around long enough to find out."

"Typical, running away to avoid consequences."

He didn't need Max to call him a coward to know that was what he was.

Zack took another drink, closed his eyes, and groaned.

The sound of Max rummaging around had Zack open an eye. "What are you doing?"

"Trying to find a calendar. I wanted to mark today as the first time in history that Zack Anderson sulked."

"Fuck you."

He'd been so busy running his life, he hadn't bothered to look for a partner for anything more than a one-night stand. Really hadn't had any interest until he'd walked into the bathroom three weeks ago and seen Nolan. "I crossed a line and I don't know why."

"He's not exactly your type."

Zack glared at him. "What's that supposed to mean?"

Max snorted. "Please. I've seen you in here. The wilder and less likely to stick around the guy appears to be, the more likely I'll find you buying him a drink."

"I haven't been on a date since . . . I prefer one-night stands. They're easier."

"Easier for who?" Max took a drink. "What's your assistant's name? Nolan, right?"

He nodded.

"Mind you I only saw him briefly, and not in the best circumstances, but he didn't strike me as one of your wild boys."

"I don't like them wild."

"I've never seen you go after a quiet one before. Never saw you look twice. So what is it about him that you're drawn to?"

"I'm *not* drawn to him."

"You kissed him."

"It was . . . You weren't there."

Zack *had* been, and even he wasn't sure why he'd kissed Nolan. No, that wasn't exactly true. When the anger had flashed in Nolan's eyes and his lips parted, Zack had been drawn to the fire he saw. Behind the obvious trauma Nolan was dealing with was a man who had more strength and presence of mind than Zack had seen. Nolan had the kind of certainty about himself that Zack had always longed for and never found. Zack had wanted to get closer to that feeling somehow . . . and he'd acted impulsively, which he tried to never do.

"Look." Max leaned forward, cupping his glass between his hands. "I don't pretend to know what's going on with you at your day job. In the past you've always looked at your boyfriends as bed warmers and your assistants as unnecessary tools."

"He's not a tool."

"Great. That means you're becoming more human. So apologize to him, or else get into bed with him. Hell, do both if you want. Being with someone doesn't have to be a distraction." Max shook his head. "Really, I think you just need to get laid."

"Piss off."

"I'm serious. When was the last time you got any?"

He wasn't going down this path. "None of your business."

"I haven't seen you pick anyone up here in months. You find out that your hot assistant is gay. You work closely with him and clearly like him."

"I'm not going to have sex with my assistant."

"Why not? You said he didn't run screaming when you kissed him. He might be up for something more."

God, he couldn't believe he was even letting his mind go there. Nolan had enough issues to deal with without adding more to the pile.

And yet . . .

"Sex would be a horrible idea. You know, the whole boss-assistant thing. HR frowns on taking advantage of subordinates." God, he didn't even sound convincing to himself.

Max chuckled. "He seems like a decent guy, and someone different would be good for you. Just promise me you'll be up front about what you want and what he can expect. He doesn't deserve to be played with. It's not fair to drag Nolan down that path if you're only going to dump him when you chicken out. But hey, consensual, no-strings sex can be fun."

Asshole. Max knew how much it pissed him off to be called out. There was no way he'd give Max the satisfaction of knowing it got to him. "You're right about one thing: I need to apologize to him."

"It's early yet. Think he's still at the office?"

"No. He was going home."

"Too bad you don't know where he lives." Max hit the desk with his hand. "Oh wait. You drove him home. You *do* know where he lives."

"Sarcasm doesn't suit you."

"It's my office. I can do and say what I want. And what I want now is for you to take this bottle, go to Nolan's place, and suck up. If he doesn't call the cops on your ass, then I suggest you see if he might be interested in an office fling. At least for the next little while until we can get the gym going and you can quit."

Zack got to his feet, taking the bottle with him. "I'm going home."

"Then leave the Scotch."

Zack tucked it under his arm. "I need to think."

"You think too much. At least when it comes to relationships."

"I'm not in a relationship." Nolan was a good man; the last thing Zack wanted was to put him in a position where he'd feel obligated to respond to unwanted advances.

Max turned back to his computer. "There's a reason you're not. At some point in your life you need to figure out why."

He stood there staring at his friend for a moment longer before leaving. "Thanks for the Scotch."

= CHAPTER =
TEN

Nolan had regretted calling Tina the moment he'd hung up the phone. Her worry had come through loud and clear, even without her saying it in so many words. It hadn't helped that she'd been in the middle of a meeting about transitioning to her new position in Vancouver. When they'd finally gotten back to the apartment, he'd been ready for her declaration before she made it.

"I'm going to tell them to give the job to someone else."

It was sad that part of him was happy to hear her say that: a small, selfish part he couldn't afford to give in to. "No."

"This isn't up for discussion." She dumped her purse on the coffee table and flopped onto the couch. "You can't ask me to leave when you're still struggling this much."

He'd gone over the words in his head nearly the entire drive home. "You're not turning down the job. You're going to tell them that you will be ready to move to Vancouver anytime." When she opened her mouth to interrupt, he held up his hand. "Let me speak."

She slumped back against the cushions. "Fine."

"I love you. You've been my best friend in the whole world since we were little. You've helped me, and I can't tell you how much I appreciate that. But now I need you to stop putting your life on hold."

"I haven't been."

"Yes, you have been for two years now." He sat down beside her, letting their knees touch. "I've been taking advantage of you, and it needs to stop. For both of our sakes."

It was strange how his breakdown today made him see just how much he'd been using his sister as a crutch. When Zack left, Nolan had been hurt, angry, and more than a little aroused. Before the accident, he would have chased after Zack, pushed him against the wall, and bitched him out before kissing him again. Today, instead of allowing himself to be the man he'd once been and handle his problems by taking action, he'd run to his sister and expected her to make the pain go away.

That wasn't the man he wanted to be.

That wasn't the person he wanted his sister to be.

Tina rolled her shoulders as if her back felt stiff, then let them drop and slumped against the couch back again. "I don't feel like I'm being taken advantage of. It was my choice to help you. Even if I feel like I'm navigating without a map sometimes."

He could practically feel the look she shot him, and they both knew the source of her frustration. It was true, Tina didn't know everything about the accident, because Nolan had decided—early on, during the air-lift to the hospital with Roberta—that he would spare his family the details of the worst part. Not the crash itself, which was all most people seemed to care about, but the twenty minutes afterward when they'd been stuck in the car, hoping against hope that they might be rescued.

His parents—his mom especially—didn't want to know much, simply happy that he was alive. His brothers teased, but had never asked too many questions. Only Tina had prodded, and even she didn't ask more than the basics. None of them knew they were asking the wrong questions; only Nolan, his psychiatrist, and his therapist knew the crash had been the least traumatic part of that day for him.

Maybe that needed to change too. Maybe Nolan had to give Tina that map, if only to prove to her how far he'd come.

He took a deep breath, released it slowly, then started. "Okay. You know the panic attacks aren't because of the injuries. And I've never told you what happened after the accident."

Tina took his hand in hers, but said nothing.

That gentle contact helped, and Nolan went on. "Before it happened, everything had been so . . . *normal*. We were talking about the session we were heading to give. Xi was still learning the material, and Roberta had been prepping him on a unit he was going to run for the first time." He could see everything perfectly. Simon sitting in the back with Roberta, teasing her about how he could time her parts of the presentation by listening for laughs at the jokes she always used. Xi in the front reviewing notes on his iPad. "Roberta took off her seat belt so she could slide forward and show Xi something on his tablet. Simon kept teasing her, said something funny and I remember laughing. It was such a typical day. The next thing . . ."

Tears welled in his eyes, and his throat tightened. Tina gave his hand a squeeze. "You don't have to."

"I do." He huffed, the air leaving his lungs with a rush. He was stalling, rehashing what Tina already knew because he didn't want to get to the scary part. "I don't remember the car spinning out. Or the impact, at least not clearly. One moment I was driving, and then the car felt like it was flying, and the next thing I remember was staring through a broken windshield at that tree in the ditch."

Tears streaked Tina's face. "Baby."

He gave her hand a squeeze, knowing if he stopped now there was no way he'd be able to start again. "From one second to the next, everything got so *not normal*. At first all I kept thinking was that I could see the bark on the tree so clearly, and I wasn't sure why. It looked too close. Because it was, since the car was smashed and the windshield was broken. Then I felt something warm on my arm, and it kind of tickled, and I looked down. It . . . Roberta's hair was brushing my hand, and the warm stuff was blood. Dripping, you know. Some of it was coming from Roberta and probably some was from my face. I didn't realize that at the time. And Xi was screaming his head off at her to wake up. Like he thought if he screamed loud enough, she'd hear him. I told him to stop, and at first he couldn't. Just couldn't. He kept looking at me over her head, with his mouth wide open like a fish. 'Waaake uuup.' And it looked ridiculous. I actually laughed. I still can't believe I did that." Xi's expression had turned to disbelief, then anger, and he'd finally snapped out of it and closed his mouth.

Tina patted his hand. "You had a severe concussion, hon. I don't think you're responsible for laughing inappropriately at a time like that."

"Yeah." Nolan shook his head. Xi had never mentioned it again, didn't seem to remember. Nolan wished he were as lucky. "So Roberta was stuck between us. We couldn't wake her up. I couldn't move, couldn't even take my seat belt off because of how the door was bent.

When I tried, I realized my leg was stuck and that it hurt. Weirdly not that much, maybe because of the head injury. Then Simon started making sounds, like he was about to throw up. I hadn't even checked on him in the backseat until then. He said something, got out of the car and hurled, and then jogged away. And it was just me and Xi and Roberta." The official report stated it had been twenty minutes from the time of the crash to the arrival of the police and EMTs. In Nolan's mind, it still stretched out to an eternity. "We couldn't tell if she was breathing or not. And everything started to freeze. The blood froze. And . . ." And then the worst of all.

"It's okay. Keep going. You need to get this off your chest."

God, she knew him so well. He shrugged. "I knew that was it. I knew that was the end, and I was going to die there. Freeze to death or bleed out. You know those grief stages?" Tina nodded, and he went on. "I think I did that whole thing in about a minute. 'This can't be happening to me. This is all a horrible dream. Damn it, it's real and it isn't fucking fair! If I make it out of this, I swear to God I'll never do anything bad again. Shit. I've wasted my life. Okay, it is what it is. There are probably worse ways to go.'" He looked at her to see how the humor was playing.

She smiled, but it looked like she was doing it to appease him. "And then the cavalry came?"

He nearly let himself off the hook, then decided to get it all over with at once. "No. Then we waited. I kept passing out, but I think only for a few seconds each time. Xi would shake my arm to wake me up. He was sure Roberta was dead, and he didn't want to be alone in the car with *two* corpses. And every time I woke up, for a split second I couldn't remember where I was or what had happened, so it was like reliving the whole thing over and over. For what felt like forever. Waking up trapped in the car, the tree trunk with snow in the ridges of the bark, the cold, the pain, something on my arm . . . and then I'd see Roberta or hear Xi and remember I was going to die."

Simon had called 911. The deathly quiet of the wooded area around the car had been broken by the sound of sirens, a crowd of first responders. Everybody yelling orders and poking at Nolan, then prying the car away from him. At some point he'd passed out again, and woke in the ambulance with the pain in his leg so bad he didn't know how he could survive it.

Phantom pain was no myth. The moment he started to think about anything that happened that day, his leg would throb. Like it was at this moment. In his mind the pain was linked to the shouts, to the throng of people who'd worked to get him free, to the sudden prickling on his forearm when Roberta's hair, sticky with half-frozen blood, had pulled away from his arm as he was taken out of the car. He hadn't realized until he was at the hospital that his face had also been lacerated when the windshield shattered. The first time he'd looked into a mirror afterward, he hadn't recognized himself.

Then had come surgery and recovery. Weeks after his final operation he'd started physio. His first attempt at talking to his therapist had started with him dissolving into a hyperventilating, frustrated, angry mess. It'd ended with him letting Tina and his other family members take charge.

Which had led him to the present time, trying to explain things to Tina that he still struggled to talk about in therapy. It hadn't been as bad as he'd feared. Kind of a relief, in fact.

She put her other hand over his, cradling his fingers and looking down at them with a slight frown. "So the panic isn't you remembering the crash, it's all the stuff that came after? Being trapped, helpless, and losing hope?"

"Oh, I remember the crash too. You know it still freaks me out when I get into a car. Not as bad as I was at first, but still." He chuckled. "I think I scared the shit out of Zack the other night about the seat belt. But it's like you said. The worst thing was being in that car forever and feeling like I would die there and I couldn't do anything about it." The physical stuff reminded him of the mental stuff, and vice versa. None of that was likely to end anytime soon, though, and he couldn't expect Tina to put her life on hold indefinitely.

"Nolan?"

He knew he had to say the words no matter how much they terrified him. "I shouldn't have called you today. I should've dealt with the issue on my own."

"I still don't even know what happened."

God, he wanted to tell her, but he didn't know what to say. Not because he didn't have the words, but because he didn't want to pull her in further. "It was just a work thing."

Tina jerked back, hurt showing on her face. "What do you mean a 'work thing'? That's never stopped you from telling me before."

"I know. But like I said, I need to learn to get through these moments. You're moving to Vancouver, and Mom and Dad don't know how to react when I get like this."

"Nolan, you know I'm—"

"Tina—"

"I might not have known all the details of what happened before now, the part of the accident that really stuck with you, but I've seen the aftermath. And the physical part alone would be enough to account for how you feel now. You still look away when you catch your reflection in a mirror, even though there's nothing wrong with you."

"Tina—"

"You push yourself too far too fast. Just like when you tried to go back to your training job. That was a call I never want to get again. For a while I thought they were going to commit you."

"I'm—"

"You didn't get out of bed for three weeks after that."

"Tina, *stop*. I don't need you to do this. I'm okay on my own."

She jerked her hands from him. "Fine."

"I'm sorry."

"No, you're not." She got to her feet and gathered her things. "Since I'm not needed, I'll go back to work."

"Tina—"

"Just don't. I need to go back to work. I left my team hanging, and they need me." Like Zack had earlier, she walked out on him.

Nolan was gutted. He knew he'd done the right thing, and that Tina would continue to put his needs before her own if he didn't give her a push to back off. He loved her and would always want and need her advice, but not at her expense. She'd worked hard to earn her promotion and would thrive in Vancouver.

What he needed to do was learn how to hold things together and get on with his life.

If that was even a thing.

What he wanted to do more than anything was to curl up in the fetal position on the couch, pull a blanket over his head, and sleep. Or, even easier, stop fighting this constant invisible battle, to let the fear and anger wash over him and simply cry. No. No, no, no, he had to fight it. Ignoring his full-body ache, he pushed himself to his feet and took a deep breath.

Focus on the here and now.

And breathe.

It was strange being home alone so early in the day, but it gave him the opportunity to relax. Needing to feel normal, he got out of his suit and found his old track pants; the comfortable ones that were well-worn from years of use. They were baggy and soft against his skin, helping to calm his emotions. The gray T-shirt was loose as well, giving him freedom to move as he liked, to stretch and come back to the moment and take stock of his needs.

Okay, he could do this now.

First thing was first—food. Not only would it help cheer him up, he could use it as a peace offering when Tina eventually forgave him and came back. Searching through the list of take-out menus by the phone, he made an order at the Indian place down the street that they both loved. They delivered, so no having to go outside, and the curry was excellent. When the doorbell rang twenty minutes later, he didn't even ask who it was and pressed the buzzer. "Come up."

He grabbed his debit card and jogged to the door when he heard the knock. "You were fast today."

When he opened the door, Nolan could only stand and stare, not entirely certain if he was having a mental breakdown, or if he was actually seeing who was waiting at his door. Not the delivery man he'd expected, but instead Zack, two take-out bags in his hands.

"I ran into your guy downstairs as he buzzed your place and paid him. I figured I owed you that much."

Nolan took the bags from him because, really, what else could he do? "Why are you here?"

"I wanted to make sure you were okay. And to apologize." He nodded toward the doorway. "May I come in?"

Nolan knew he should say no. Really, this shouldn't even be a consideration in the realm of things that might happen in life. Nothing good could come of having Zack in his home looking crestfallen and a bit ragged. Was that Scotch he smelled? "Have you been drinking?"

"I didn't drive here if that's what you're worried about."

"I never thought you would." He squeezed the plastic bag handles, the weight of the food starting to dig into his palms. Tina would be home sooner rather than later, and he didn't want any reason for her to be more upset than she already was. Having Zack here would certainly get her prodding him about what had happed to Nolan earlier to set him off. That conversation wouldn't end well.

But when he looked into Zack's eyes and saw that the normal flashing spark was gone, he couldn't help but step aside. "I ordered enough for two."

"I won't stay that long." Zack closed the door and took off his shoes. "Is your sister home?"

"No. She had to get back to work." *Because work is the cure-all for pissed-off sisters.*

"That's a lot of food for one person."

"I was going to suck up to her with leftovers."

It was strange having Zack in his home. Normally Zack was larger than life, filling any space he entered so there was barely any room left for the air. But here in the apartment, Zack seemed smaller. No less potent, but more contained, as though he was holding himself back. "So you came to make sure I was okay. I'm here. I'm fine."

Zack nodded. "I'm glad."

Nolan set the food on the counter and waited while Zack searched for whatever he was trying to say. The silence stretched on too long and threatened to restart the tension in Nolan's chest. Sucking in a breath, he shook his head. "Can I get you something? Water? Coffee?"

"A second chance."

He froze. "Pardon?"

For the first time since Zack had offered him the position, he looked as though he didn't know what to say. "Last month I was tasked with the job of reducing the operating budget by fifteen percent. Funny enough, it was the same day I hired you. I need to find ways to cut technology costs, or else Compass will be left with no choice but to cut employees."

"Oh."

Zack nodded. "I've been trying to find a way to do just that. There isn't a lot of fat to trim, but I refuse to give in, not when the livelihood of our staff is at stake. I ran into Chopra this morning after my meeting with Rollins. He demanded that I look at his proposal, that it would save the company millions. He was loud, obstinate, and drew attention. Samantha wanted to know why I hadn't followed up with this, given what she'd mandated. This morning she told me that I have three weeks to come up with a plan or else she's going to announce cuts at the next all-hands meeting."

Nolan would have been furious as well. "I'm the reason Chopra was so confident that you'd listen to him."

"You were, but that didn't give me the right to take it out on you, especially when you didn't know the full story. That said, I could use your help." Zack ran his hand through his hair, making it stand up the way it had earlier that day. "I need an objective eye to review the information. If Chopra's proposal is sound—and the kickback thing isn't an issue—then I'll bring it forward. If it isn't workable, I need a plan B."

There was something about Zack, the way he held himself, that told Nolan more was wrong. If they'd had this conversation this morning—before Nancy and her cupcake, before being yelled at, before being kissed—then he might have been more inclined to reach out, to ask what was the matter. But so much had transpired in such a short time, Nolan knew he needed to hold back. To pace himself and not get into a situation he couldn't handle.

"I need you. I need you in the office." Zack came closer but stopped before they were in kissing range. He cleared his throat; his gaze sliding from Nolan's to roam his face, looking for who knew what. "Will you come back to work tomorrow? Will you help me?"

"Yes." Nolan was surprised his voice didn't crack from the weight of sudden emotion he was forced to suppress.

"Will you forgive me for earlier? For yelling?"

"Yes."

Zack stepped near, so tantalizingly close Nolan could have swayed and been once more chest to chest with him. "Will you come out to supper with me?"

Nolan blinked. "What?"

"While this smells amazing, I promise you I can do better." A smile tugged at Zack's lips. "I know it's only five, but we can get an early meal. Then, if I haven't scared you off, I'd like to show you something."

Shit. This was too much for him. The wave of emotions was more than he could take. When he had to simply think of Zack as his hardheaded boss, it was easier to deal with the man. But this? It didn't compute. "My sister will be home soon." A lie, but one he needed to preserve his sanity.

"Another time, then. I don't think she'll want to see the man who upset her brother."

Tina would probably tackle-hug Zack if she suspected he was starting to get to Nolan in a way no other man had before. "Good idea."

Neither of them moved. Nolan's gaze dipped to Zack's mouth, and the memories of their brief kiss came racing back. He'd still been so overwhelmed from the anxiety that he hadn't fully appreciated the gravity of what they'd shared. He'd kissed the dragon and he'd survived.

Not only that, he'd enjoyed it.

"I should go." Zack's voice barely reached above a whisper.

"You don't have to." Nolan felt the blush cover his cheeks. "I think supper might be good."

Zack's eyes flashed. "Your sister? Won't she expect you to be here?"

"Currently she's pissed at me. I was exaggerating a bit before. I don't expect to see her for hours."

Zack nodded. "Do you mind driving, or would you rather take transit?"

"I don't own a car."

"Taxi it is." Zack shoved his hand into his pockets. "Let's go, then."

= CHAPTER =
ELEVEN

Zack knew it would have made no sense, but he should have insisted they take the bus instead. He hadn't expected that being in such close proximity to Nolan would impact him the way it did. This was the second time Nolan had sat in a car with him, but the first time side by side. They'd come miles away from that Friday night at Frantic when he'd fallen apart, overwhelmed by his anxiety. With only the notable exception of earlier today, Nolan had been able to deal with his challenges amazingly well.

Zack didn't want to stare, but he found it hard to keep his eyes from the handsome man beside him. Given how nervous Nolan was in cars, Zack didn't want to give him any further reason to be upset.

"Are you okay?" Nolan turned in his seat to face him.

"Yes. Why?"

"You're acting weird, and I don't like it."

"Sorry to offend you, Mr. Carmichael."

"I'm not offended." He shifted back, but Zack knew he was still watching him. It was uncanny how he was able to do that.

"I really am fine. I was thinking."

"About what?"

"You." It was Zack's turn to stare at his companion. Nolan squirmed in his seat, as he looked out the window. "I was thinking about how far you've come in such a short time with the company. With no experience as an assistant, you righted my office. I never did thank you for that."

"You're welcome." Nolan sniffed and rubbed his hand along the top of his left thigh.

The red light was long, as was the line of cars in front of them. They should have walked, been outside in the cool evening air.

It wouldn't have lent to conversation, not as intimate at any rate. That might have been safer. Zack drummed his fingers on the seat between them. "I never did ask what you trained? Technology? HR sessions?"

Nolan shifted forward once more, his eyes shining a bit brighter than they ought to in the night. "I worked with insurance brokers. Trained them on soft skills mostly. How to talk to clients, how to get to agreements in negotiations with difficult personalities. Conflict management, sensitivity training, that sort of thing."

"So you were training people how to deal with assholes. Like me."

"Pretty much."

The light turned green and traffic began to move. "Do you miss it?"

"The assholes? No, I have you."

Zack glared at him. "Training?"

"Yeah. I do. Every day, actually."

He could have pressed further, but he didn't want to hurt Nolan any more than he already had. "The restaurant is just up ahead."

The Pear Tree was packed, groups of people hovering around the hostess area. Zack had a standing reservation, and thankfully didn't have to wait. He recognized the hostess who was working that night, and she smiled as he came in with Nolan a few paces behind him.

"Hello, Mr. Anderson. We're glad you were able to make it tonight. Just the two of you this evening?"

"Yes, May. Thank you."

"This way, please."

A guitar duo played softly on a small stage in the corner of the restaurant, the light melody underscoring the relaxed atmosphere. May led them to his normal spot, a small table in the corner opposite the musicians. It was far enough away from the kitchen that there wasn't an endless parade of people passing by, but close enough to the bar for him to get quick refills.

"Here you go, gentlemen. Carlo will be by shortly to take your orders."

Nolan hadn't said anything since their arrival, an unusually long silence for him. Zack waited until May finished filling their water glasses and sauntered away before he turned to his date.

No. No, not date.

His friend. His valued employee.

"The menu is standard fare. Since Compass is paying the bill, I'd suggest getting the braised short ribs as an appetizer and the Kobe burger with chorizo sausage. Excellent."

Nolan was looking around, a frown marring his face. "Why are we here?"

"I thought we'd established that back at your place. This was a chance for me to apologize for being a jerk." It didn't matter that the opportunity to spend time with him outside the office was more appealing than it should be. "If you'd rather go someplace else, I'm fine with that."

"You had a reservation?"

"I have a standing reservation here. Well, three nights a week. It's close to home for me, the food is good, and I like the company, even if I don't talk to anyone."

Nolan cocked his head to the side, his lips parted as though he might ask something. Of course that was the moment the waiter arrived to relay the daily specials. Zack did his best to hide his annoyance. It wasn't Carlo's fault that he'd interrupted a chance for Nolan to get to know Zack, to ask him questions that had nothing to do with appointments or proposals.

It was an opportunity for them to connect as people. Two men, a bit lonely, a bit broken, who'd had some success in life but still yearned for something more.

"Do you want the usual, Mr. Anderson?"

"Please. And I'll have water to drink."

"Make that two. And I'll have the Ultimate burger. Well-done. Thanks." Nolan pulled his loosened tie free from around his neck and stuffed it into his pocket.

Fuck.

Nolan looked around the restaurant, his eyes wide. "This doesn't really seem like the sort of place I'd expect you to come. Especially to eat alone."

"Why's that?" The Pear Tree was a mix of modern and traditional. Wood, metal, and good music playing every night. And while it was busy most nights, the noise never rose to uncomfortable levels.

"It's almost . . . casual. Relaxed." Nolan thumbed the sweating water glass in front of him. "Not words I'd associate with you."

It shouldn't have upset him, hearing what Nolan thought of him. It wasn't anything he hadn't heard from others before. Still, annoyance rose up to tighten his chest. "No. I guess not."

Nolan cringed. "Sorry. I didn't mean to offend—"

"No." Zack closed his eyes and took a few calming breaths. "You're right. I guess the truth of the matter is I like coming here sometimes instead of eating at home because I get to absorb some of that relaxation. I've gotten better at dealing with my anger issues over the years, but there's always room for improvement."

The waiter came back with their waters, forcing Zack to bite back words he probably shouldn't say. He liked the restaurant, but he'd be lying if he said he liked coming to the Pear Tree alone all the time. He hated seeing the pity in the eyes of the staff every time he confirmed it would be "just one" for dinner. Again. He hated that he couldn't seem to get past this emotional block that prevented him from developing any sort of meaningful relationship.

Instead of an ill-timed confession, he drank.

Nolan followed suit, and the silence that fell over them was underscored by the buzz of chatter from the other patrons. Zack didn't want to start the conversation again, didn't have a clue what to say that didn't involve work or peppering Nolan with questions about his accident. They might have shared a heated, ill-advised kiss, but that didn't give him the right to delve into Nolan's obviously painful past.

"So how did you find this place? There are a lot of restaurants around here. This is on a side street. It wouldn't be someplace you'd just stumble on. Unless you spent a lot of time searching for hip joints."

Zack snorted. "You sounded like my dad right then."

"Well, the silence thing was getting awkward. All of my practiced small talk revolves around training humor, which believe me you don't want me to lead with." Nolan shrugged. "So, how did you find this place?"

The answer would require Zack to reveal a part of his life no one else at work knew anything about. Not even Samantha. While it wasn't anything that would damage his reputation, it inevitably changed how others saw him. Keeping quiet about it for so long had also made it *feel* like a secret, and it was hard to overcome the habit of avoiding the topic completely.

Nolan held his gaze, his expression growing more curious and amused the longer the silence stretched on.

Clearing his throat, Zack swallowed down some beer to boost his courage. "I go to a gym around the corner. I found this place when I was walking from there back to work late one night. Heard the music, didn't really want to do anything at the office, and decided to wander in here instead."

The wrinkles around Nolan's eyes as he frowned made him look even cuter than normal. "There's a gym around here?"

Zack forced his hands to relax; he knew once he went down this road there was only one logical conclusion. "It's a boxing gym."

"I had no idea. Mind you, I tend to stick to my own little part of Toronto most days. Is it a busy spot? And wait, you box?"

"I learned how to take a punch when I was a kid." It was strange, the way Zack's heart pounded at the thought of telling Nolan. Shit, even his hands were sweating. He was given a small reprieve when their food arrived, Nolan's burger and his steak.

Nolan was apparently starving, the way he dug immediately into the food. The sounds of pleasure coming from him were obscene, and eventually Zack couldn't resist a dig. "Should I leave the two of you alone?"

Nolan waved his hand. "This is the best ever. So glad you brought me here."

In a flash, the tension that had built to near painful proportions dissolved. Zack smiled and allowed himself a few moments to savor his steak. "See, I know what I'm talking about."

Nolan nodded with an enthusiasm that he'd rarely seen in another adult. "Hey, is that gym open? Given the caliber of this place, I feel like you have pretty good taste. Maybe I should be looking at going there instead of the weight room in Tina's building. I mean, not that I'd be much of a boxer with my bad leg and stuff, but my doctor has been after me to do more strength training. Mixing it up might be better than using the same weight machines all the time."

There was no reason to think Nolan would betray his trust if he showed him. No reason to believe anything horrible would come from opening the door of his personal life just a tiny crack to share with someone else. He'd already shared so much with his assistant—no, his friend—that this was the next natural step.

Wasn't it?

"Are you okay?" Nolan wiped a hand on his napkin and gave Zack's hand a pat. "You zoned out there."

"I'm good. Just thinking."

Nolan grunted and picked up his burger again. "You need to stop working all the time. I would be surprised if your brain ever shut off."

"It does. Sometimes." Fuck it, why would he have brought Nolan here, if not to visit Ringside when they were done? People had interests outside work that they shared with friends. There was no reason to chicken out now. "When you finish up I'll take you over there."

"Awesome." Nolan licked a fleck of ketchup from the corner of his mouth. "Should be fun."

Fun. Yes, it could be fun, or it could change everything. Zack took another bite of steak, this time tasting nothing.

Nolan was clearly a thick idiot. Either that or the food had been so unbelievably amazing that it had cast a spell over him and changed his perspective of the world around him. The building he currently stood in front of was not at all what he'd been expecting. There weren't any flashing lights to advertise it, no sweaty, hulking men and women streaming in and out.

Hell, there didn't appear to be any windows.

"I thought you said this was a gym?"

Zack stood in front of the door, fiddling with a padlock. "It is. Was. Will be."

"That made about as much sense as Chopra's technical budget."

If there'd been a sign in front of the business, it was long gone. Fluorescent tubes buzzed above them, but the marquee itself was devoid of text. Zack was oblivious to Nolan as he finally opened the lock and pulled the old door open, dislodging a handful of paint flakes. "Let me get the alarm first."

"You have a security alarm in this place? Wait, why do you know the code? Why do you have a key?"

The mono-melodic sound of electronic buttons being pressed gave way to silence, then clicking as Zack flicked on light switches. "I own the building."

Nolan's mouth fell open, and his feet refused to move. "What?"

"Get in here and I'll explain."

The air inside was thick with dust and no doubt three different types of mold. The space he'd entered was large enough to accommodate the large central boxing ring, several side areas where people could work out, and some punching bags along the back. There were mirrors around the walls, though many were either broken or so dirty they were useless. Nolan had never been in a place like this, but by the way Zack moved to the ring and climbed inside, he was clearly no stranger.

"So." Nolan shook his head. "You own a defunct boxing gym."

Zack leaned his forearms on the top rope and nodded. "I do. It took every penny I had to buy it, which didn't leave me much to spend on renovation."

"You said, 'It is. Was. Will be.' Explain."

He'd gotten to know Zack's moods quite well over the past month. He'd seen him frustrated, impressed, annoyed, and once even pleased. He'd never seen him nervous.

Zack looked around, a soft smile on his lips. "I know this will come as a surprise to you, but I wasn't the best teenager."

"No?" He rolled his eyes. "And?"

"*And* my parents were at their wits' end most days dealing with me. I was angry, lost my shit around them on more occasions than I'd care to admit." He turned his head, making it difficult for Nolan to see his face. "My parents got me into therapy, and the therapist suggested the afterschool boxing club here at Ringside. Russel, the owner, had a grandson who was gay and had been bullied so badly in high school that he eventually . . . well. Killed himself. In his memory, Russel started this club for LGBTQ kids to learn self-protection, but also how to deal with frustration. Channel our anger and fears into something that wouldn't get us into trouble. At first it was just a few of his grandson's friends, then word spread and it turned into kind of a haven. It gave us a place to hang out where we could feel accepted and talk to other kids who were going through the same stuff. I came here three times a week and worked out my teen angst on a punching bag. Once I learned some control, I graduated to boxing with people."

It was so easy to see Zack as an angry youth. The tight control he had over his emotions at the office, his difficulty dealing with his assistants, it all made sense. "You've come a long way."

"Not far enough. I'm not a nice man, but I could have grown up to be far worse. This place helped me get a handle on my feelings. When Russel passed away, the gym shut down. That was seven years ago, and ever since it's been a dream of mine to open it back up. To make it available to teens who need a safe place to blow off some steam."

"So why are you working for Compass? It sounds like this is your passion, your dream. Why not quit and do this full-time?"

"Money." The way he said the word, it was as though a needle of steel had pierced him.

Of course. Taking another look around, Nolan began to guestimate the expenses. So much had been worn down from time, neglect, or both, leaving very little that seemed salvageable. "Is the ring in good shape?"

"It's the only thing that's giving me hope. The rest will have to be fixed, probably gutted in some areas, like the showers and steam room. I'm sure most of the building isn't up to current building codes either, so that would be significant. I need investors to help not only with the setup, but with the ongoing costs for paying instructors and doing the initial promotion. My hope is for the teen program to be free, supported by the regular members or maybe a government grant."

Nolan came farther into the room, trying to picture it full of boxers, seeing a young and angry Zack in the ring trying to learn self-discipline. "How many other kids were part of the program?"

"Most of the time I was here, the group was at a low point, and there were only two others. You met Max the other night, he owns Frantic. Eli is our other buddy, but he moved out to Calgary a few years ago. We weren't the first teens this place helped, and there were many after. The numbers fluctuated, but Russel took in anybody who wanted to come and was willing to follow the gym rules."

Nolan looked where Zack pointed, to a faded poster on the wall. The paper was water-stained, and the lower half of the page had been torn off. He could barely make out the words on a few lines:

2) If the manager is wrong, refer to rule 1.

3) Don't forget your towel. Use it!

4) Put all equipment back in the proper place after use.

Nolan smiled to think of Zack and his friends, and tons of other kids over the years, policing each other on replacing weights and wiping down sweaty benches. Caring for the place that gave them an escape from more serious concerns. He could only imagine how special this place had been to so many. No wonder Zack wanted to bring it back to life.

"I've never been in an old-school gym like this. Or a boxing ring. I'm not exactly the athletic type." Ignoring the dirt on the ropes and the pain in his leg, Nolan carefully climbed up into the ring. "What can I do to help?"

"Nothing."

Nolan snorted. "Please. You can't undertake a project of this magnitude alone. I've seen your work calendar, remember. You'll need someone to do some running around for you, set up meetings with city inspectors, get an estimate for construction costs—"

"No."

"You need to have an estimate for something like this before you can approach investors. They'll want to—"

"I said *no*."

Nolan snapped his mouth shut and turned to face Zack. This shouldn't be a big deal. He might be new to being an assistant, he might not know everything he needed to if he was going to help with this, but he wasn't an idiot. He'd proven himself capable. But before he could open his mouth to say any of that, he looked Zack in the eyes.

Instead of the cocksure executive he'd grown used to, there stood a man who appeared to be stripped of all defenses. If Nolan didn't know any better, he'd have thought Zack was scared, or at the very least unsure of what to do next. That wasn't the man he'd come to know over the past month.

That said, he knew he wasn't the most perceptive of people lately. He'd gone through so much in the last few years that he'd kind of become blind to other people's problems. Stuck in a mire of uncertainty for months on end, working through both physical and emotional pain, never knowing if the next thing he'd do would set off his anxiety, he'd drawn his focus inward and it was hard to reverse that.

But not with Zack. Nolan had come to know his moods, to understand his underlying currents. This uncertainty was so out of character for him, Nolan could only assume that the gym meant more to Zack than he would acknowledge.

Looking down at his feet, Nolan bounced a bit on the canvas. "This isn't exactly as I pictured it being. It's harder than I realized."

"You need something that's firm underfoot but able to cushion your fall when you go down."

"I'd be on my ass a lot." Taking some larger than normal steps, he did his best imitation of a boxer, landing awkward punches on floating dust motes. "God, I'd suck at this."

"Most people do when they first start. Once you get some training, it can be a great way to get out your frustrations and get into shape."

Nolan couldn't imagine taking up a sport that involved him hitting people—even before the accident, he'd never have thought to try it. "I'm more of a lover than a fighter."

"Don't know about that, but you're not a bad kisser." Zack laughed when he looked over at him. "You're cute when you're surprised."

"I'm not." The ache in his leg started up, and he reached down to rub at it.

"Are you in pain?"

"A bit. It sometimes happens at the end of a long day." His physiotherapist had warned him there was only so much they could do to get him back to normal. The pain would always be a part of his life, and he was learning to manage it as best he could. He'd made a point not to complain. When he did slip up and mention it, Tina tended to fuss over him, but Zack . . .

Zack was his boss.

"Never play poker." Zack made his way across the canvas, looking as comfortable on the surface as Nolan felt awkward. "Every thought you have flits across your face for the world to see."

Nolan cringed. "Yes, I learned that the hard way." With only a short distance between them, Zack's warmth and scent wrapped around him. "Don't think I don't know you've totally changed the subject. I could be a big help, and it looks like you need it."

"You changed the subject, actually. I can't bring you into this, Nolan. I . . . You're not . . ." Zack growled. "You're my employee. Asking you to work on this place is so outside the acceptable range of what's appropriate, even I can't justify it."

Nolan couldn't be certain, but there seemed more to Zack's dismissal than Nolan simply being his employee. He seemed almost protective of the gym. Or maybe of himself. "You didn't ask. I offered. I assume your plan is to help other LGBTQ teens? Not just the ones who need it for anger management?"

"That was the plan. Max wanted to have a girls-only group as well. His sister spent a lot of time here in high school, and she'd make a great coach."

Nolan found himself taking another step closer, shrinking the nominal space between them even more. "See, then that is something I'd want to be a part of. I'm not asking to be a joint owner or anything. I don't have the money for that. But this place could be important and help a lot of people. I'm more than happy to volunteer my time to get it going."

Zack's gaze slipped from Nolan's to land on his mouth. "You're going to do all that on top of helping me with the problems at Compass? You'd be stretched too thin, and I need you focused at work."

Nolan's heart raced, and he had to swallow hard before he could get the rest out. God, this was the sort of thing that he'd longed to be a part of for years, even before the accident. He wanted to contribute, to touch the lives of people who struggled, make things better, make things *right*. "I know you might find this hard to believe, but I think I could be a real help to you . . . to the gym. I want to."

The air between them was warm, heavy with unspoken words and charged with sexual tension. With something else, too, that was new to Nolan. He didn't just want Zack for sex, but to spend time with. He wanted to keep conversing, keep bantering, even if it was more intense than he was used to. He loved that Zack never treated him with kid gloves, despite having witnessed more than one of his attacks; he didn't baby Nolan or think he couldn't do his job.

Then there had been the kiss, and the dinner. Clearly at least some aspects of the attraction were reciprocal, and if Zack didn't want to be around Nolan more, he wouldn't have invited him to share a meal.

It didn't make sense that Zack didn't want him involved with this. Did it?

Zack took another step so there was barely an inch separating them; he reached up and cupped the back of Nolan's head, but didn't pull him in for the kiss Nolan desperately wanted. Their eyes locked, and Nolan lost all awareness of everything else around them. The truth was, Zack had become the center of his life in such a short time he was completely overwhelmed; that alone should probably have made him wary, but it didn't.

Fighting his impulses to *kiss, touch, grab,* Nolan instead whispered, "Let me help you."

Zack cupped the back of Nolan's head with his other hand. "I'm scared of what that would mean."

"Whatever you need it to mean."

"I'm not a nice man."

"I'm a broken man. We seem to get along just fine."

"This is different." Zack's eyes slipped closed for a moment as he sighed. "I don't want to break you any more than you are."

"You won't."

"You don't know that. I could. I've already pushed you to the edge once. I wouldn't want to do that again."

Jesus, what a stubborn ass. Nolan leaned in so his lips brushed Zack's. "You also pulled me back from the edge. Twice." Closing his eyes, he kissed Zack softly.

Zack's fingers flexed against the back of Nolan's head, but didn't move him any more. Nolan could feel his body shaking through those simple points of contact, knowing Zack was holding back. It was fine, this was good. The gentle pressure of lips and fingers only highlighted the passion Nolan knew simmered below the surface. He knew how good things were when the longing exploded, but it was equally good to experience the gentle side of Zack.

Wanting to tease, he dipped his tongue out and ran it along the seam of Zack's lips. He did it again until Zack relented and opened his mouth. Fingers tightened in his hair. Nolan's cock hardened as he rubbed against Zack's. Memories of their all too brief previous kiss roared back, sending his arousal through the roof.

Mutual pants, gasps, and the sound of the canvas creaking beneath their feet filled Nolan's ears. Zack was warm as Nolan moved his fingers beneath his suit jacket to run along the folds of his dress shirt. He wanted this man like he hadn't wanted anyone in years. It was wrong and amazing and all the things Nolan didn't think he'd ever experience again.

Zack slid one of his hands from Nolan's head down to his back and moved him even closer. The move was enough that it forced Nolan to put his bad leg at an awkward angle.

The breath he sucked in at the bolt of pain was unexpected, and Zack immediately pulled back. "Are you okay?"

"Fine. Keep kissing."

"That wasn't *fine*. What happened?"

No, no, no, he didn't want to get into this. "My leg. It's fine. Keep kissing."

When Zack stepped away completely, Nolan groaned his displeasure. "You've mentioned your leg before."

"I have."

"Are you okay?"

"I was in a car accident. A pretty major one. I'm lucky to be alive, and I'm just fine dealing with a bad leg." He hadn't been naked with another man since he'd been injured, and hadn't a clue how someone would react to seeing the mangled white skin. He wasn't exactly freaked out about it, but he wasn't in a rush to be judged harshly either.

Not that he thought Zack would.

If they ever got to that point.

"Can we go back to the kissing?" He batted his eyes for good measure. "I liked the kissing."

The second Zack frowned, Nolan knew the moment had passed. Zack dropped his hands. "I better get you home. I'm sure your sister is back and wondering where you are."

Nolan gathered this wasn't going to be an *I better get you home so I can get you naked* thing. "Probably. Don't want to be tired and piss my boss off tomorrow."

Zack snorted and moved to hold the ropes up for Nolan to leave the ring. "I hear you work for a real jerk."

"He can be when he's stubborn. I know how to settle him down though." Nolan slid beneath the ropes, but not carefully enough. The moment his feet hit the floor, he realized that something had fallen onto his jacket. Expecting to see dust, a startled shout exploded from him when he looked down and saw a spider. "Fucking hell!"

Furiously, he beat at his shoulder, spinning around to make sure he'd gotten the spawn of Satan as far away from him as possible. The pain in his leg was nothing compared to his loathing of spiders. When he saw the little bugger trying to scurry away, Nolan stomped near it just to make certain it wasn't going to turn back.

Panting, he looked up to see Zack staring down at him from the ring, eye squeezed shut and face red. Nolan swayed toward him, but stopped for fear of getting closer to the spider. "Are you okay?"

Laughter exploded from Zack as he gripped the top rope with both hands. He gasped and nodded and then laughed some more.

Nolan couldn't stop from rolling his eyes. "Yes. I'm scared of spiders. Blame my eldest brother for that."

"The look . . . on . . . your face!" Zack tried to stop long enough to get himself out of the ring, but failed. "Spiders!"

It was weird, Nolan normally got annoyed whenever someone teased him about his fear. He wasn't thrilled to be a fully grown man terrified of such a tiny creature, and hated when he was reminded of his failing. But seeing Zack—hard, angry, serious Zack—laughing uncontrollably, Nolan felt his heart swell. "I thought you were taking me home?"

"I am." Zack wiped tears from his eyes and took a deep breath. "Sorry."

"Don't be." Nolan reached over and punched his shoulder. "There, we're even."

They fell into step and headed toward the door. "If you're going to help out here, you're going to have to get over that. There are a lot of spiders around this place."

"I promise to do better." Nolan grinned. "So, you'll let me help?"

"I'll use you as spider bait."

Nolan punched his arm again.

Zack shook his head, and seemed to come to terms with something. "I could use the company getting this place up and running."

Nolan knew something had changed between them, small but significant. The way they walked together, relaxed. The sexual tension was still present, but had wrapped its arms around their budding camaraderie. They were becoming more than boss and employee, or accidental kissers. They were becoming friends.

Nolan took a deep breath as they stepped outside into the Toronto night air. "Good. We'll get started tomorrow."

= CHAPTER =
TWELVE

Zack hadn't slept much after he'd gotten home that night. He'd been hard as a rock from the moment Nolan had slipped into his car until well after he'd dropped him off at his apartment. He'd tried most of the night to get Nolan out of his mind. Jerking off hadn't helped; neither had reviewing work documents. Maybe Max was right and he'd been on his own too long. Either that or he was under more stress than he realized.

Or he could accept the more obvious explanation. He liked Nolan in a manner that went beyond professional respect. The attraction had been little more than physical when he'd first laid eyes on him, but after a month of working side by side with him, Zack knew it had grown past that. He'd let his guard down, and the strangest part was that Nolan wasn't even his type.

Maybe that was *why* he hadn't kept his emotional dukes up: he hadn't expected Nolan to have that kind of impact. And now, Nolan had managed to insert himself in nearly every crack of Zack's life without him fully realizing. Even the gym would no longer offer a safe haven from the attractive, funny, caring man . . .

Fuck.

What had really broken through the last of his barriers was the spider.

Dear God the spider.

His lips stretched into a smile each time his mind replayed the events. The look of horror on Nolan's face as he tried to destroy the tiny arachnid was forever burned into Zack's memory. Zack hadn't laughed that way in years. Hadn't thrown his head back and let loose a giant belly laugh.

It was a good feeling, something he'd like to experience again. That was the main reason for his purchase on his way home the previous night and his utter excitement waiting for Nolan to arrive this morning.

Yeah, he was an asshole.

The soft sucking noise of the glass office door opening sent a thrill through him. It took great effort to keep his gaze locked on his computer monitor instead of on Nolan as he strode into the office.

Nolan popped his head into Zack's office. "Good morning."

"Morning."

"Need a coffee refill?"

"Please." He held out his mug without making eye contact. "I've been here awhile."

"Need me to get anything together for you?"

"Just the coffee, please."

The moment Nolan turned the corner, Zack grinned. He wasn't *this* person, not the one to buy gifts and certainly not the one to play pranks. The gurgle and pop of the coffeemaker spitting out a fresh cup sent his heart beating. It took real effort to school his features in time for Nolan to return with the mug.

"Here you go." Nolan set the coffee down in front of Zack's keyboard before pausing. "Are you okay?"

"Yup, just trying to finish this report." *Don't smile. He'll know something's up.*

"Okay." Nolan frowned and looked back at him twice before moving over to his desk.

Zack did his best to watch without looking too obvious. Nolan went through his usual routine, setting his own coffee down, picking up the jacket he'd slung across the reception counter, hanging it up carefully, and returning to the coffee to take a slow sip as he subtly stretched out his leg.

Finally, he pulled out his chair, and—

"*Fuck!*"

Zack burst out laughing.

"You asshole!" Nolan picked up the giant stuffed spider that Zack'd found at the toy store and shook it at him accusingly. "Asshole."

"But it's so cute and fuzzy. I thought you and Ralph could become friends."

"Ralph. Who the hell names a spider Ralph?"

"The manufacturer. It's what was on the tag. Check the recycling bin if you don't believe me."

"I can't believe you did that to me." Nolan threw Ralph at him, and Zack barely caught it in time.

Zack threw it back, still chuckling. "I can't believe you actually called me an asshole. *Twice*. Consider Ralph therapy to help you get over your phobia. I told you, there are a lot of spiders at the gym."

The dramatic glare and eye roll Nolan threw his way were more than enough to relax him. This was the reaction he'd been hoping for—playful and accepting. A positive start to a work day that might end up more than a little stressful.

Taking a sip of his coffee, Zack returned his attention to the top of his email list. After he read the first few lines, the happy vibes he'd been cruising on evaporated.

Shit.

He'd been handling a discipline issue with one of his managers for a few months now. Complaints of inappropriate comments toward female employees and poor job performance. In this day and age, Zack kept hoping these incidents would become old news; the sad reality was that even with Compass's clear policies, frequent trainings, and track record of zero tolerance, this shit still happened all the time.

He fired off an email to Nancy, knowing she'd have to be involved with the inevitable termination. Before he hit Send he glanced over at Nolan, who'd slid Ralph to the side of his desk in full view of Zack. Three pens were now in Ralph's grasp, as though he were Nolan's adorable little helper. The thought revived Zack's smile. No matter how bad his day might get, there were small things he could hold on to, things that would make him happy.

Things like Nolan.

And Ralph.

Zack picked up his phone and dialed the HR extension, then listened through the chipper greeting before responding. "Good morning, Nancy."

"Mr. Anderson?"

"Yes. You sound surprised."

"No. Of course not." She paused. "Are you okay?"

Zack pulled the receiver away from his head and looked down at it for a moment before responding. "Yes."

"Oh good. You just sounded different."

"Different how?"

"Ummm, happy. I guess." She cleared her throat. "Can I help you with something?"

"Ryan Cooper. He's been on a PIP for about three months. I received another performance complaint."

"Oh God, not more inappropriate comments."

"Thankfully, no. He screwed up another deal by missing a deadline."

"I assume you want to start termination?"

"How soon can we get rid of him?"

"Well, with the performance plan, I'd ideally like to get things documented. I need a few days to do the paperwork. It's Wednesday and I hate to terminate right before the weekend. Can we do it on Tuesday morning? My schedule's clear around nine thirty."

Zack wanted the asshole gone as quickly as possible, but he trusted Nancy to do her job. "Sure. We'll do it in my office."

"I'll get Janice to start the paperwork."

One more thing done at work. One more problem solved for Compass. One more step away from accomplishing his goal of leaving the company and reopening Ringside. A few months ago, it might have bothered him more than it did today. Back then, he didn't have Nolan around to make the days manageable, enjoyable.

Not that making him laugh should be part of the job. But something about Nolan felt so inviting that Zack forgot about professionalism around him. Let that guard down, because Nolan wasn't just attractive but also *got* him. Still... when Zack made himself stop to think about it, was he really any different from Ryan Cooper?

He'd never intentionally said anything to make Nolan feel uncomfortable, and he certainly hadn't suggested that Nolan's job depended on anything that fell outside the scope of the written position description. But neither had he really checked to make sure his attentions were wanted. Not in so many words. Nolan had seemed to be on the same page, but maybe Zack was making too many assumptions.

Shit, maybe he wasn't any different.

Nolan took a pen from Ralph and gave it a little pat on the head before turning to make a note. He was efficient, and could play the serious business professional well, but there was always an undercurrent of something more lighthearted. Whimsy, even. He had been through so much, was still working through a lot of it, but he somehow managed to have a positive outlook. Maybe Max was right, and that was exactly the appeal. Nolan might not be Zack's usual type, but he could smile and laugh and find the humor in just about any situation. Zack hadn't realized how much he'd been missing that kind of lightness in his life.

Maybe there was a chance.

Maybe.

He pushed those thoughts away and went back to work.

When Nolan arrived a bit later than usual Thursday morning, the light from Zack's office was already on. Zack was head down, poring over a number of reports, when Nolan hung up his coat and went to the kitchenette to start the coffee. There were no "good mornings" or heated glances. Nothing to indicate that anything unusual had happened between them. That they hadn't shared not one but two kisses, plus the exchange of a novelty plush spider. That Nolan hadn't spent the last two days wondering what it would be like to go to bed with Zack.

He'd been worried things would change after the gym—that Zack, despite his words, would treat him differently. But Zack ignoring him was business as usual, and the tension he held in his shoulders lessened. He knew how to act professional, so if that was how Zack wanted to play things, Nolan had it covered.

He waited for the coffee to finish brewing, filled them each a cup, and went to face the dragon. "Good morning, Zack."

"Nolan." He didn't look up.

"You have an eight o'clock appointment this morning with Jennings and Burk from purchasing, a conference call with the London office at ten, and it's your mother's birthday."

Zack looked up at that. "No, it's not. Her birthday is in March."

"Just making sure you're paying attention." He somehow managed to not smile. It was cute to see Zack so peeved. "Is there anything I can get for you?" *Blowjob? Handjob?* Okay, this was going to be harder than he'd thought.

"I'm fine, thanks."

"I'll be at my desk if you need me. Ralph and I have reports to read over." He did smile then, but didn't linger any longer than usual.

With Zack not needing him to do anything urgent, Nolan set about reviewing their calendars. He had a doctor's appointment coming up in the next week that he might have to postpone if Zack's meeting this morning resulted in an updated production schedule. He also had lunch planned with Nancy, and he didn't want to reschedule on her again if he could help it.

Zack's agenda for the coming week included all the regularly scheduled meetings, one conference call, and Ryan Cooper's termination meeting—Nolan probably wasn't supposed to know what that meeting was about, but it hadn't been hard to piece together.

And that was it.

Boring for a Thursday morning.

He tried not to look over at Zack, but he could see him from the corner of his eye. Nolan normally didn't mind the mornings when it was this quiet; the silence was a rare pleasure and usually meant Zack was in a good mood.

He opened his email and looked at the first meeting request. Mr. Chopra again. Yeah, that wasn't happening until the budget information had been reviewed and Zack had an action plan. He sent a generic response and closed the email. When Zack coughed, Nolan turned his head. For a moment he thought his boss was going to say something, but Zack didn't look up. Nolan stared at his email, but didn't open the next one. Zack cleared his throat again and shifted in his chair. Nolan did his best to ignore the fantasies of what he imagined it would be like to have him pressed against his body.

And there was a cock twitch.

Bad times.

Nolan jumped from his chair, and Zack looked up. "You okay?"

Great, now Zack was going to worry that Nolan was about to have another anxiety attack. "I'm fine. Just realized the time. I'm going to be late for some training." Nancy had been after him to complete the workplace health and safety session since his first week. The weekly orientation session was due to start, so he wasn't even lying.

"When will you be back?"

Odd, he'd never cared about Nolan's schedule before now.

"An hour. Maybe more. Not sure how long these HR things go." Zack held his gaze until Nolan felt his cheeks flush. "Don't forget your eight o'clock."

"Say hi to Nancy for me."

He fled, praying Zack couldn't see the tented front of his pants.

He stayed away for a total of two and a half hours. It turned out there'd been a large roundup of delinquent employees who'd missed the training that week, and the session was packed. The moment he sat down, he regretted his impulsive flight. Janice was the trainer, and to say she was awful would be generous. Nolan might not be able to lead a training himself anymore, but he still knew how it should be done, so he was keenly aware of exactly how Janice was failing to engage her audience.

To make matters worse, his anxiety made it nearly impossible for him to stay in the room. Instead of sitting, he ended up standing by the door, ducking out periodically when he felt as though the walls were closing in around him. Once the session was officially over and everyone filed out, Janice made him stay and complete the mandatory test in the empty room.

That wasn't the least bit embarrassing. Not at all.

By the time he made it back to the office, he was drained. For the second time since he'd started working at Compass, he wasn't sure he'd be able to make it through the day. Life had a way of making other things happen. He was greeted by the sound of voices as he stepped back into their space.

"Nolan!" The edge was in Zack's voice. "Come here."

"Yes, Mr. Anderson." He wasn't familiar with the man who occupied the guest seat. "Is there something I can get for you?"

"Your assistant is a man?" The man snorted, making it look as though his horrendous burgundy tie were choking him. "You got shortchanged, Anderson. You don't even get a nice ass to look at."

Zack's face was stone. "Nolan, I need you to get sign-off on the two forms I left in a folder on your desk. Do that now."

"Of course." There was something about the way Zack stood, about the aura of disgust and anger that rolled off him in waves, that put Nolan on high alert.

Before he could turn and leave, Zack held his gaze. "Shut the door behind you, please."

He nodded but frowned. Zack gave his head a small shake, so small that Nolan doubted his guest even noticed. Nolan's stomach soured as he began to put the pieces together. The door clicked shut, muting the voices on the other side. When he opened the file folder and saw the termination notice, he didn't need to hear what was being said to know what the words would be.

Shit. This wasn't going to go well, he just knew it.

He dialed HR. "Hi, Nancy."

"Hey, dragon slayer. I heard you finally went to the health and safety training. Thanks for that."

"Sorry, this is a time-sensitive call. Zack is doing a termination right now, and I think we might need security."

"Oh no. Who is it?"

He couldn't recall the name, so he scanned the form. "Ryan Cooper from development."

"Shit. Shit, shit, shit. Is he in there *now*?" He'd never heard Nancy get frantic before. "He promised me he'd wait until next week."

The rise of voices on the other side of the door only served to underscore his concern. "Yes, he is. And it sounds heated."

"Security is on the way. I'll make sure that we deactivate his badge and lock out his computer access. Shit, why didn't he wait for this?"

"I was in training. They were here when I got back. Not sure what happened."

"Okay, they're coming. Just keep an eye out in case something happens."

"Fuck you!" There was no mistaking that.

"Too late." He hung up on Nancy, knowing she'd get help here as quickly as possible.

Cooper jerked open the door, but rather than head for the exit, he came straight at Nolan. "Fuck you too!"

He got to his feet and backed away. "Mr. Cooper, security is on their way up. If you would please head toward the elevator, they'll meet you there to escort you from the building."

"You're his little toady, aren't you? Piece of shit bootlicker! I'm going to fuck you up."

Nolan stood paralyzed. The scenario unfolded in slow motion in his brain. One moment Cooper was coming at him, and in the next Zack was spinning him around, redirecting his attack. He saw Cooper pull his arm back and swing at Zack. Watched in horror as his fist connected with Zack's jaw, sending him falling to the floor in a heap.

"Zack!" He moved without thought, getting between them. "Back the hell off!"

Cooper kicked at Zack but connected with Nolan's injured thigh instead. He cried out, tears instantly welling as pain sliced through him, but he refused to move away from a near-stunned Zack.

There was a sudden flurry of activity. Three security guards rushed into the office and pulled Cooper off Nolan. He heard Nancy and Janice talking to people, asking him questions. The only thing he was able to focus on was Zack. Reaching down, he helped him to a sitting position, and touched the already visible bruise on his jaw. "Are you okay?"

Zack groaned and gave his head a small shake. "I should be asking you that."

"I'm good. You took a big blow. You should get checked out for a concussion."

"I told you I can take a punch. I'm fine." Zack looked past him. "Nancy, I want to state for the record that I have no plans whatsoever to fire my assistant. Ever."

"I'm very happy to hear that, Mr. Anderson." She moved to squat beside them. "We'll notify the police so they can get charges started. Now if you two men will do me the favor of coming to the hospital with me, I want to make sure that you're both going to be okay."

"No need. He barely touched me." Nolan was sure his grimace gave away how much pain he was in, but the last place he ever wanted to go was the hospital.

Zack nodded. "I just need an ice pack."

"I learned in health and safety training today that there should be one in the freezer. Let me get it. And I thought you said you were a good boxer?"

"He caught me off guard, or else I wouldn't have taken that punch. I'm normally much faster." Zack rubbed his jaw. "I'll have to get back in the ring again with Max and brush up."

Nancy looked between them. "You two are the most stubborn . . . I'm glad you're working together."

"I'm just glad Nolan took my training this morning." Janice chuckled as she dropped the ice pack into Zack's lap. Nolan was shocked to see her smiling at all. "Come on. Let them lick their wounds."

The office emptied out, leaving the pair of them still sitting on the floor. Nolan shifted away from Zack a bit, moving so he could lean against the wall. "Never a dull moment."

"Nope." Zack pressed the pack to his jaw and hissed. "Asshole got me good."

"Next time you're going to fire someone, wait until I've got security in the wings."

"I couldn't. I've been working with HR to get rid of him for months now. I finally got the last nail this morning and needed to slam it in the coffin."

"What was that?"

"He'd been harassing one of my managers. She'd finally filed a report with the company and informed me she was going to be pressing charges. I wanted him out of the building as soon as possible. No one should have to work in conditions where they don't feel safe. Or sexually harassed."

Nolan shook his head. "No."

They sat there side by side as the insanity of the last few minutes dissipated. Nolan's leg throbbed in a way it hadn't since the early days after his accident. He'd have to get in the tub that evening and let the hot water work its magic.

Zack cleared his throat. "You don't, do you?"

He looked at him. "Don't what?"

"Feel unsafe or harassed? I know I've crossed a line. We've kissed and I'm your boss. I don't want you to feel you can't say no, or that you have to put up with unwanted attention."

The uncertainty was painful to hear. "No, not at all." He placed his hand on Zack's thigh. "I don't know, maybe it shouldn't happen again, but I don't feel pressured. I don't . . . regret what happened."

With his free hand, Zack reached out and covered Nolan's. "I'm harsh, but I'm not unfeeling. If you need anything, if your anxiety gets to be too much, or if I'm riding you too hard, just say something. I really do appreciate what you've done for me since you started. I can't imagine going back to working alone."

Zack smiled, and Nolan's heart raced at the sight. His chest felt tight, but not from fear or anxiety. No, this was gratitude and something a bit stronger than respect. "Thank you."

"We better get off the floor if we're going back to normal."

"Probably for the best." Nolan struggled to his feet and offered a hand to Zack. "I'm going to order us some lunch. I think we've earned it."

"Can you get something from that Indian place you ordered from the other night when I stopped by? I haven't been able to stop thinking about it. Smelled amazing."

═ CHAPTER ═
THIRTEEN

For the first time in months, Nolan was up on a Saturday morning before noon. Tina had gaped at him as he wandered into the kitchen wearing track pants and a T-shirt. He'd taken a bit of perverse pleasure in stealing her Pop-Tart.

"You're awake. And dressed." She shook her head. "Please tell me you're not going into the office. Especially dressed like that."

"I'm not going into the office. And what's wrong with the way I'm dressed?"

"Nothing if you were going for the upscale-hobo look."

He was in fact meeting Zack at Ringside to do an inventory of needed structural changes. Nolan had volunteered to coordinate with Max to find a list of contractors and get estimates, so they'd know exactly what funds they would need to move forward. Why they hadn't done this before now, Nolan hadn't a clue.

"You're smirking." Tina reclaimed the last piece of her Pop-Tart and ate it before he could stop her. "Normally that means you're meeting a man you have a crush on. Since you're not dating anyone, I know *that* can't be it. So where are you off to?"

Under normal circumstances, Nolan would have told Tina everything. But they still weren't back to normal since their sort-of fight. He didn't want to give her any reason to regret accepting the Vancouver job. So he offered her only part of the truth. "I'm actually off to do some volunteer work."

Tina smiled at him and for the first time in days looked more like her old self. "Really? That's awesome. Where?"

"It's an old gym they're trying to get up and running again. They also want to offer LGBTQ youth programs. Boxing, self-defense, and stuff."

"You're not doing anything too labor intensive right? I know you need to be more active, but they shouldn't make you lift boxes, or—"

"Tina, I'm fine."

The tension snapped back into place like a whip. "Sure. I'll be here looking for apartments online. They want me to fast track my move."

That stopped him. "What? When?"

"Next week if possible. They offered to put me up in a hotel until I find a place that suits. It's going to be a bit harder than I realized, though. Rent is high."

He wanted Tina to go, needed her to, even. But next week? "What about your things?"

"I'll have to keep them here for the time being. Don't worry, I won't cramp your style for long."

"Don't be like that."

She turned back to the computer. "Call if you need me."

"I will." The peace he'd felt mere moments ago was gone. "I have to catch the bus." Not wanting to drag things out further, he kissed her quickly on the cheek and bolted for the door.

The trip down to Ringside was uneventful. The buses were on time and weren't overly crowded. He even had a chance to swing by Starbucks and grab some coffees and pastries to go. So when he pushed open the heavy metal door to the defunct gym, his body was relaxed and ready to face the day.

He immediately stopped when he saw Zack pulling a large blue mat across the floor. He was dressed in jeans and a tight-fitting T-shirt. The fabric hugged him perfectly, accentuating exactly how fit Zack truly was.

And yeah, he was pretty frigging fit.

Nolan hoped his track pants were loose enough to hide his erection.

"You're late." Zack's voice echoed through the room. "But I smell coffee, so you're forgiven."

No man had the right to be that hot. "I took a chance and grabbed some lemon cake too. It was pretty fresh and I really love it, so that's my excuse." Shit, now he was rambling. "Want it now?"

"Sec."

Nolan was then subjected to watching Zack pull the clearly heavy mat to the side door and toss it onto a heap of other garbage. Sweat made Zack's hair stick up in a way that shouldn't be attractive and yet totally was. Nolan closed his eyes and counted back from ten—the first time he'd done this as a way to calm his libido rather than his nerves. He had barely gotten to one when Zack's scent washed over him. He opened his eyes, smiled, and handed him the coffee.

"Careful, it's hot." *Like you!* His inner teen laughed.

Zack gave him a strange look before accepting the coffee and taking a sip. "Thanks."

Get your mind back on task. "You look like you've been here a while already."

"My Saturdays have a way of going sideways. If I'm coming here, I like to get an early start in case I have to take off."

There was most definitely something different about casual Zack, something more than a simple change of clothing. The lines around his eyes and mouth were relaxed, and he didn't hold himself as stiffly. Nolan swayed closer as he responded in kind. "So, where do you want to start?"

Zack's gaze drifted to Nolan's mouth before he turned away and took another sip of coffee. "Let's make a broad list of areas we want the contractor to tackle. We can break it down from there."

Was that a shut down? It had been so long since Nolan had dipped his toes into the dating waters, he rightly didn't know anymore. It shouldn't matter. He wasn't here to engage in any sort of relationship with Zack, only to help him get Ringside up and running. A little volunteer work to pay things forward.

Certainly not to take advantage of the situation to ogle his boss and maybe friend in his oh-so-tight jeans. That had nothing to do with the reason he was . . . Dear God, Zack's biceps were huge.

Shit.

This was going to be harder than he thought.

It took a while for Nolan to get his head in the game, but after a few minutes they'd both finished their coffees and were working side by side, making notes and inspecting the facilities.

"I can't believe you and Max haven't done this by now. No point in trying to get financial backers if you don't know how much things are going to cost."

Zack picked up a decayed wooden bench and moved it against the closest wall. "Max has his plate full with Frantic. It took me a long time to get the money to buy the building in the first place. On top of what I do at Compass, I don't have a lot of spare time."

"Fair enough."

Zack stopped and leaned back against the wall to look at him. "Besides, this is more my project than Max's. He wants it open again, but if it didn't, he'd simply find another way to give back. I'm the one who wants to do this full-time."

It was strange, but Nolan could picture Zack wandering through the clean halls of Ringside, pausing to help a kid or answer questions from one of the trainers. The frustration that seemed to propel him forward through the halls of Compass wouldn't be there.

Nolan could see Zack being happy here.

He wanted something like that for himself. He wanted to have a life of his own again, wanted to find someone who wouldn't mind his occasional freak-out. He needed a man who had flaws of his own, but wanted to be better. They could help one another, be a support system for one another, like what his parents shared.

For the first time since his accident, Nolan *knew* what he wanted. He knew that this was only going to happen if he was brave enough to reach out and take it. Zack might have been the one to kiss him before, but Nolan would have to make the next move if he wanted something more than that.

Zack pushed away from the wall. "You okay?"

No. "Yes. Just thinking."

"About what?"

"You. Specifically kissing you."

The muscle in Zack's jaw jumped. "I'm your boss. That's probably not a good idea."

"What if I think it is? A good idea. What then?"

Zack's gaze traveled down Nolan. "I wouldn't want you to feel pressured. I'm no better than Cooper if I think you're doing this for any reason other than wanting to."

Nolan continued closer, each step making his cock swell and his heart pound. "I'll make you a deal."

"What's that?"

Nolan took one final step so no space existed between them, closed his eyes, and leaned forward. "Until Monday morning, I quit."

And then he kissed Zack.

Zack's brain shut down as his mouth opened to accept Nolan's. He didn't need to think or worry about what was right or wrong. The only thing that mattered was the man in front of him and their mutual pleasure. Zack did the thing he'd been wanting to since he'd walked into the bathroom that first day and saw Nolan. Pushing his hand into his hair, he tugged Nolan's head back and licked a long swipe up the side of his neck.

The groan that burst from Nolan was worth the throbbing that pounded through his neglected cock. Sliding the other hand beneath Nolan's shirt, Zack bit the side of his neck. "I've fantasized about fucking you against the wall for days now."

The shudder that passed through Nolan was more than Zack could have hoped for. He wasn't normally a fan of track pants, but on Nolan it gave him the freedom a suit and tie wouldn't allow. Not only could he rub his thumb across Nolan's nipples, but there was little to hide Nolan's thickening erection from him. It was good, perfect. He needed to know that Nolan wanted this as much as he did. That he wasn't forcing himself on him. That was the last thing he wanted to do.

"Zack," Nolan moaned, his hands clutching at Zack's back. "Please."

"Shit." Zack ground his hips against Nolan's, pressing their cocks together. "I don't have anything." Condoms were the last thing he'd had on his mind when he'd gotten to Ringside that morning. This wasn't supposed to be about sex; they were supposed to be working. For the kids!

Nolan chuckled. "Me either."

"We're not very well prepared, are we?"

"I'm sure as hell not. I haven't had sex in two years."

Zack pulled back to look him right in the eyes. "What?"

Nolan smiled. "Not a priority when you can barely walk and can't go out into public."

"Right." No protection meant no penetration. That didn't necessarily mean no orgasms. "Do you trust me?"

Nolan looked at him, and for a moment he wasn't sure what the other man was thinking. His heart pounded hard when Nolan finally nodded.

"Good. Relax."

He let go and spun them both around so Nolan's back was pressed against the wall and Zack was now the one calling the shots. Yes, this was how he'd pictured him: flushed and wanting more. Zack slipped one hand around the back of Nolan's head, and the other one around his hip. It had been a long time since he'd done this, not since he was a teenager. Back then he wasn't experienced enough to be good at mastering the technique. That wasn't the case now.

Holding Nolan still, Zack began to thrust his hips forward so their groins pressed together briefly before pulling back. The kiss of their cocks, that blessed contact, was enough to steal his breath away. Another thrust, this time met halfway by Nolan. Zack couldn't breathe, didn't care if he ever breathed again. Over and over they thrust, not quite grinding together, as the pleasure built.

"God," Nolan said on a sigh.

"Yeah."

"I haven't ever done this."

"Good." Zack couldn't explain why, but he was happy he was the first one to do this with him. Nolan had been through so much, and while he didn't know much about the man who'd become an unexpected part of his life, he couldn't help but want to be the one to share this experience with him.

The rhythm they set was slow and steady. Pleasure rolled through Zack gradually at first, infecting one inch of his body at a time. It didn't take long for his clothing to feel restrictive. Thank God he had on a T-shirt. He'd be choking in anything else. It took time, but they synced up: breathing, thrusts, pants. Zack closed his eyes, but tried to memorize everything he felt. The smell of Nolan, the sounds he made as their mutual arousal grew.

Zack turned his face so his mouth was pressed just below Nolan's ear. "I shouldn't want to, but I keep picturing you naked, spread on my bed. I wonder what you'd sound like, feel like. How tight your ass would be around my cock."

Nolan groaned. "Yes."

"Yeah, you'd like that. You'd want to feel me slide into you. Spread you wide, your cock trapped between us. Wouldn't you?"

"Yes."

Zack tightened his grip on Nolan's hip, slowing his bucking. "No, not yet."

"Please."

"No. Slow."

Nolan banged his head against the wall. "Asshole."

"That's me." He bit Nolan's neck as he reached between them to squeeze Nolan's cock. "I bet you're wet in there. Leaking. I'm tempted to shove my hand in there to see, to feel you." Instead he squeezed Nolan's shaft through the soft fabric. "Next time. Right now I want to make you come like this. I want you to cream your pants so that every time you put these on you think about me."

"I wanna—"

"That's it. Do it for me." Zack took hold of Nolan's hips in each hand and thrust as though there were no tomorrow. He wanted to hear and feel him come. He wanted to blast away the anxiety that seemed to rule Nolan's life.

Nolan's body tensed, his muscles shuddering in Zack's grip. His breathing came out in shorter and shorter gasps, until Zack wasn't sure how he kept from passing out. Nolan bit down on his bottom lip and banged his head hard against the wall.

"Fuck."

"Come for me."

Nolan shook his head.

"Do it now. Right now." Zack increased the pressure between them, to the point where he didn't think he'd be able to hold back much longer himself. He wished they could be closer, naked somewhere. It hadn't been long, only minutes since they'd started, but he was already planning for a next time. His world was changing.

He sought Nolan's mouth and sucked on his bottom lip, raking his teeth across the plump flesh. Nolan dug his fingers into Zack's shoulders, flexing and clinging, holding on tighter the closer he got to orgasm. His body was vibrating, and for a moment Zack thought it would never come, that they'd be stuck on this precipice forever, dancing on a knife's edge between desire and oblivion.

And then, finally, Nolan lost their mutual rhythm. He cried out, his body shivering as his fingers locked in a death grip on Zack's shoulders. Triumph spurred Zack on; no longer focused on Nolan's pleasure, he was able to lose himself in his own. He pressed his nose to the side of Nolan's neck and ground hard and fast against him. The press of soft lips to his temple, the gentle kiss that silently encouraged him on, were all it took.

Hot come flooded his underwear as he groaned long and loud. The pleasure exorcised everything that had haunted him that week. It rolled down his spine, infecting every inch of him with warmth, an unexpected sense of peace.

As quickly as their frantic coupling had started, it was over. He still had Nolan pressed against the wall, his face was still against Nolan's neck. Nolan's hand found Zack's hair; he teased the strands just above his ear.

"So that happened." Nolan's voice was soft, sleepy. A lover's voice. A lover?

Zack pulled back and let his gaze drop to Nolan's groin. The gray cotton was now dark, wet with his come. Without thinking, Zack reached inside Nolan's pants and threaded his fingers through his come-soaked pubic hair, teasing his softening cock. "It did happen." He swallowed. "We really didn't think this through. You need clean pants."

"Damn." Nolan closed his eyes with his head resting against the wall, his body relaxed. "You don't happen to have any spare clothing?"

"I might have a pair of sweats in my gym bag. Let me check." When Zack pushed away, he instantly missed Nolan's warmth. "I'll be back in a minute."

Nolan couldn't get rid of his giddy, stupid grin. He'd read lots online about frottage, but he hadn't really tried it before. Not on purpose, to completion. Going forward, he would have to correct that oversight.

He and Zack.

It had been an odd and unlikely partnership from the moment they'd met in the bathroom, and yet here they were, engaging in something more than a working relationship. Was this a fling? He'd never had one of those either. Zack was introducing him to all sorts of new things.

His leg was starting to throb, and he had no choice but to sit down on the worn-out bench Zack had dragged over earlier. He hadn't noticed the pain while they were making out—having sex?— but that was good. He hadn't worried about his appearance either, about what his body looked like or if Zack would hate any scars he saw. It had been over two years, but Nolan was beginning to feel like himself again.

By the time Zack finally returned from wherever he'd kept his stuff, Nolan's orgasm buzz had started to wane. Maybe they could do something else. Maybe . . . "Were you able to find anything?"

"Just a pair of shorts." He held them out, but didn't quite meet Nolan's gaze. "I wasn't sure if you'd want them."

And in a flash, all of his confidence evaporated. Letting Zack see his leg would have been hard. Letting the world see it was something he couldn't even contemplate. "No. That's okay."

Zack sighed. "You'd rather walk around with come stains than put on shorts?"

"Yes." Nolan looked down at the floor, letting his hair slip forward to cover his eyes. "It'll dry and I'll be fine before I have to leave."

Zack paused far too long before he spoke again. "This was good." His tone suggested otherwise.

"It was good, but . . . ?"

"We probably shouldn't do it again."

Nolan's head snapped up, a mix of anger and fear shooting through him. "Why not?

It was Zack's turn to look away. "I'm your boss."

"I told you that isn't an issue. Not for me at least."

"I've also never done relationships. Not serious ones. Things always get heated, fights happen, I leave." Zack scanned the bench, the wall, the shorts he still held in one hand; his gaze never settled long. "I don't want anything to ruin what we have, our working relationship. Or our friendship."

"It won't." Nolan swallowed hard. "But I won't beg. If you're not interested, then we'll consider this a one-off and forget about it."

Zack pinched the bridge of his nose. "Monday. We'll talk then. I need to think in the meantime."

The joy Nolan had felt since the moment he'd walked through the doors of Ringside fizzled. "Is there anything else you need help with today?"

Zack shook his head. "I'm fine."

Nolan pushed himself to his feet, took the shorts, and pulled them over his pants to cover the come stain. "Well, I'll look like an idiot, but that will hide the evidence until I get home. I'll see you Monday."

He walked away, ignoring as Zack called out his name.

The trip home was as awkward and uncomfortable as the journey to Ringside had been smooth and full of nervous anticipation. Strangers eyed his shorts at the bus stops, on the bus. His leg throbbed, and the chill from his wet briefs didn't help.

He took an extra-long shower as soon as he got home; there really was nothing more challenging than cleaning dried come out of your pubic hairs. He didn't mind though, because the hot water eased the pain, which helped clear his mind so he could think about what he and Zack had done at the gym.

Zack was right that it shouldn't happen again. Zack was wild, unpredictable, and so determined to maintain power and control, he couldn't function in a scenario where he didn't control the outcome. Faced with an unpleasant truth he couldn't alter—Nolan had a disfigured leg he would never feel comfortable displaying in shorts—Zack had withdrawn his affection and interest. He hadn't even bothered to come up with an original excuse; his "I don't want to ruin our friendship" was one of the oldest brush-off lines in the book. The part about his relationships always ending in fights and him leaving had been just as clichéd, but probably accurate.

In the short time Nolan had worked for Zack, he'd learned his boss always found a way to pull the strings in any situation. Nolan was one of his resources at work, a tool he could use to help him control his world and make every business transaction play out the way he wanted. Nolan's mistake had been thinking things were any different outside the office. Zack had gotten exactly what he wanted out of Nolan, but pulled back immediately when the focus shifted away from gym renovations or getting off.

Nolan couldn't get involved with a man who was self-centered. In the end, he knew he'd be left behind, discarded when he was no longer needed.

He had too much respect for himself to accept a relationship like that.

Turning the water off, he stepped out of the shower and turned to face the mirror. Even covered with steam, he could still see his broken body reflected back. He'd been relieved when Zack hadn't had a condom, sparing them both the inevitable shock of Zack's seeing his scars.

As he had so many times since the first day he was free from splints, casts, and bandages, Nolan ran a finger along the gnarled fissure of scar tissue crisscrossing his thigh. The skin was white, angry looking, rough, and ragged where metal had torn flesh. Muscle was irreparably damaged, making physio a constant in his life. Tracing the path up toward his flaccid cock, he tried to imagine how Zack would have reacted had his fingers moved a few inches down and to the left. Would he have ignored the scar, dismissed it as an anomaly? Would he have asked? Wanted to see what was there? Asked how long, how deep it went? Wanted to know how it felt when they'd pulled the door off him and drawn the metal out of his skin?

Nolan turned his face, no longer able to look at himself. He hadn't had a lover since the accident. Despite Tina's assurances that a boyfriend wouldn't care about something like this, it was hard to get past. He'd woken up more than a few times covered in sweat, heart racing as imaginary laughter of a dream lover echoed in his head.

No, Zack was right. It was better for both of them if they never let this happen again. Nolan had enough to deal with, without adding a doomed love affair to the mix. Monday he'd go to work, do his job, and forget this moment ever happened.

CHAPTER FOURTEEN

Zack had spent nearly every moment since Nolan walked away thinking about him. The look on Nolan's face as the happiness bled from it and was replaced with hurt continued to haunt him. He regretted his words the moment he'd spoken them, knowing they were tactless, even if they weren't angry. He'd taken that moment—a special and spontaneous memory—and twisted it with a few words.

He might have been a brute in the ring, but his words had always packed more power than any punch.

Nolan was already at his desk when Zack arrived at the office. He had no doubt Nolan saw him the moment the elevator doors slid open, which meant the cold shoulder was intentional. Nolan gave him a tight smile as he walked by to his office, but that was all the acknowledgment he received.

Well, what did he expect? He'd taken advantage of Nolan on Saturday—pushed him against the wall and rubbed off. It didn't matter that the kisses were mutual, passionate. Zack shouldn't have let Nolan's casual appearance and relaxed mood seduce him the way it had.

And yet . . .

Max was right: he was a coward. There were ways he and Nolan could handle a workplace relationship. He could get Nolan transferred to another executive, or have Nancy in HR figure something out. Then there'd be no reason they couldn't do what they wanted, when they wanted.

He picked up his pen, turned his chair directly at Nolan, and stared. Nolan's back straightened, but he said nothing.

Leaning forward so his forearms rested on the desk, Zack began to tap his pen on the blotter. Nolan shifted in his seat, the force of his typing echoing louder in the office.

Zack tapped his pen on his empty coffee mug.

Nolan turned his head in a manner that would have made the cut in *The Exorcist*. "Is there something you need, Zack?"

Zack tapped the edge of his mug again. "A coffee."

"I brewed a fresh pot twenty minutes ago. Lots there." Nolan smiled and turned his attention back to his computer.

Ouch.

"I deserve that." Zack got up and grabbed his mug. On his way by Nolan, he grabbed *his* mug as well. "I don't know how you take it."

"Cream, three sugars."

Zack made a gagging noise as he turned the corner. "That's not coffee."

"Been drinking it that way since I was twelve. It's just fine."

He cringed as he defiled the coffee with sugar. "You're better off drinking pop."

When he returned to the office with the two cups of coffee, Nolan had turned his chair around, his arms crossed. "I have a sweet tooth."

"Well, here." Zack held out the mug. "I hope this is okay."

It was strange, but Zack didn't remember ever getting one of his assistants coffee before. Shit, he didn't remember doing anything kind for any of them. He should have been more considerate; it had nothing to do with role, position, or authority, but rather decency.

Nolan reclaimed his mug and frowned at Zack before he took a sip. "Thank you."

"You're welcome." Zack slipped his hand into his pocket. "And I'm sorry."

"You have nothing to apologize—"

"Yes, I do, and you know it. You didn't deserve being pushed away like that. I . . ." He shook his head. "You might find this hard to believe, but I don't have a lot of relationship experience."

"What, a prize like you? The men should be beating your doors down." The normal bite to Nolan's words wasn't there. He looked down into the mug. "Sorry."

"I earned that. Probably more."

"Maybe." Nolan snorted. "I was surprised."

"About the sex?"

"About your wanting anything to do with me. I know I'm not the most attractive of men since my accident."

The hell? "What are you talking about?"

Nolan set his mug on the desk, and his hand dropped to his left thigh. "My face never healed quite right. My nose is crooked, and I have facial scars that aren't pretty."

"None that I can see." Zack had no idea Nolan was so self-conscious.

Nolan's eyes were wide; strands of his hair covered most of the left side of his face down to his cheekbone. He pointed to the long forelock, which Zack had always assumed was a deliberate, edgy style choice. "The hair is more than a fashion statement."

The air around them changed, growing heavy, still. Zack stepped closer and really looked at Nolan, tried to see the imperfections that caused him so much pain. No, his nose wasn't entirely straight, but it wasn't so crooked as to distract from the rich hazel of his eyes. When his eyebrows were both visible, it was clear that one drooped slightly, giving him the appearance of a man always assessing, always thinking of a snappy comeback. His mouth was perfection: full lips that Zack wanted nothing more than to kiss there and then. "There's not a thing wrong with you."

Nolan's lips tightened into a thin line. "That's naive and hurtful."

"You said you weren't attractive any longer. My comment was directed at that statement, not your injuries."

"You have no idea what it's like to look at yourself in the mirror and hate what you see." Nolan stood, leaving little space between them. "You have no idea what it's like to pass by that mirror in the lobby every day, catch a glimpse of yourself, and not recognize that it's you. To continuously hear screams in your head whenever you sit too long and suddenly your leg and back cramp up until you can't breathe for the pain."

Zack wanted nothing more than to wrap Nolan in his arms and hold him, but given the look on Nolan's face, he knew the gesture wouldn't be appreciated. "You're right. I don't. I only know the man who's overcome so much in a short period of time. I see you set your mind to a task, whether you know how to do it or not, and get things done. You're kind and funny and smart, and you might struggle, but you don't let it control your life. I don't think if I lived through what you did that I would've come out the other side as half the man I see standing before me."

Nolan's gaze slipped away as he gripped the edge of his desk. "I'm broken."

"No, you're different. I might not know all the details, but you went through something horrific. That'll change you." He reached out for Nolan's hair, pausing long enough to telegraph his actions and give Nolan time to stop him. When he didn't, Zack lifted the fringe and looked at the ragged scar that ran along the edge of his hairline. "This isn't ugly. It's proof of life. Would it help you to tell me how it happened?"

Nolan opened his mouth, breathed in as if to speak, then closed it again and shook his head. "No . . . I'd rather not. Maybe sometime."

Zack was surprised at a pang of disappointment, but he shrugged it off. "Your call, but I still say it means you survived." He let the hair fall back into place and went to his office. "So, what's my first meeting this morning?"

Nolan was still standing where he'd left him, even as Zack reclaimed his seat. Zack watched as Nolan's shaking hand reached up and tucked his hair behind his ear, then pulled a thick hank forward to mask the side of his forehead again. "You have a call with Chris at the UK office."

"Thank you." Zack's heart raced as he dialed the extension.

The rest of the morning was spent with Zack trying to not let Nolan notice he was looking at him, and Nolan playing with Ralph. The tension between them still simmered, but it had changed into something different. He'd probably said the wrong thing and offended Nolan. If that was the case, then he'd apologize again and offer to find him a new position.

Which was the last thing he wanted.

Shortly before noon, Zack glanced up to see Nolan's entire demeanor change. Gone was the pensive, soulful expression, replaced with tension. Ralph was set down on his desk and Nolan was quickly straightening his things. That wasn't normal for him—

The door whooshed open, and Nolan smiled. "Good morning, Ms. Rollins. How may I help you?"

Shit.

Zack got to his feet, all semblance of peace having evaporated in a flash, and met his boss at his office door. "Samantha. I'm surprised to see you today."

Ignoring Nolan, she pushed past Zack into his office. "We need to talk. Privately."

"Of course." Zack cast a quick glance at Nolan, who was already on his computer, no doubt trying to figure out what was going on.

Samantha wasn't a woman who stood on ceremony, nor was she a person who pulled any punches. When Zack turned to face her after closing his door, he wasn't completely surprised to see steel in her gaze.

"What's going on?"

"We have a problem, Zack."

"Budgets for hardware purchases for the next quarter will be done by the end of the week."

Samantha closed her eyes and sighed. "Don't worry about that for now. We have a bigger issue that needs to be addressed."

He moved to his desk and sat down on the edge. "What's going on?"

"The finance team was going through the books, part of their quarterly audit. They found a number of discrepancies when it came to some tech purchase orders. Further investigation showed line items listed and bought that didn't match purchase requests."

Zack's team was responsible for the company's technical purchases, but there wasn't a centralized process for oversight. Any manager on any team could buy something IT related through the regular requisition system, and he had no way to know if a tech order had been made until it was reported to him during quarterly accounting. "I told you, we should have a dedicated purchasing department for this sort of thing. Not everyone knows what they're doing or exactly what they're ordering. If I had to personally research and approve every order, I'd never have time to do anything else."

"That doesn't help with our immediate concerns."

"Which is what?" Unfortunately, he had quite the imagination when it came to this sort of thing. So many ways for problems to arise and go sideways on them.

"Finance thinks one or more of our vendors might be scamming us. They need someone with technical expertise to go through POs from the past year to identify any problems. If this runs as deep as I think it might, we'll be suing."

It was a good thing he was sitting down, because the amount of work she'd suggested was staggering. Tech orders included everything from specialized equipment and server arrays right down to printer cartridges and thumb drives. "*Every* PO for tech? That would take an entire team of my staff at least a month."

"You have a week."

"Samantha, that's not—"

"One week."

"What about the budget?"

"Still due Friday."

What a nightmare. "Do you have any idea what you're asking me to do?"

If she felt bad about the situation, Samantha didn't show it. "Get a conference room, order food for them, do what's necessary to get the facts. I need to know how deep this thing runs, and I need to crush it fast." She gave him one final look before leaving.

Nolan was sitting at his desk, his eyes glued on Samantha as she bolted through the main office. He waited for the door to close before turning his head to Zack.

"I spoke with Kyle down in Operations, and he gave me some of the details. A purchasing scam?"

"We need to find out if this is a mistake, if a vendor has been defrauding us, or if someone on the inside is arranging this for a kickback."

Nolan groaned. "How long did she give you?"

"One week."

"Shit." He turned and began typing on his computer. "I'll book a conference room and clear your calendar."

Zack shook his head. "We also need to get the budget done. Same time frame."

God, he hated this, being the only one who seemed to be able to solve a fucking problem in this company. Exhaustion would be the least of his concerns given how much he needed to do. Not to mention that he wouldn't have a moment to get anything done on the gym, which meant Max would be saddled with anything that came up.

Nolan pushed away from his desk and came into Zack's office. "We'll work out a plan to get it done. Not that I have training in any of this, but you won't have to worry about the organizing or running around."

A small measure of relief washed over him. "Good."

Zack's cell phone rang. Fishing it out of his pocket, he saw Max's name on the display and accepted the call. "Not a good day, buddy."

"Yeah, kind of shitty on my end too. It might get better, though, if things line up. I think I've found a contractor who'd be willing to work with us at a discount. Something about having kids from a high school carpentry class acting as apprentices. Don't know, but it's worth checking out."

"I'll have to leave it to you. I'm going to be locked in the office for the next week."

"Shit. Really?"

"What?"

"I can't. I have to hop on a plane in two hours and head to Calgary for at least a week. Mom's in the hospital. Her appendix burst, and I need to be there for a few days to help her at home."

"Your dad can't help her?"

"Apparently his new arthritis meds are hurting more than helping. He can barely get out of bed. They need me there."

Zack reached up and pinched the bridge of his nose. "Then let's reschedule with the contractor."

"Can't. He only has these kids for a limited time, and if we go ahead with it, there's a significant amount of paperwork that needs to happen beforehand. If we don't get the ball rolling in the next few days, then we lose the kids, which means we get pushed to the back of his queue."

Zack jumped at the gentle touch of Nolan's hand on his shoulder. "You need my help."

"No, I'm—"

"I've got you."

How could three simple words make such a huge difference?

"Was that Nolan?" The humor in Max's voice came through loud and clear.

"Yes."

Before Zack could stop him, Nolan took the cell out of his hand. "Max? Hey, yeah . . . Better, thanks. If you email Zack the information, I'll grab it and make the arrangements . . . No problem at all. I think the gym is a worthwhile cause. I hope your mom is feeling better soon . . . Okay, perfect. I'll go get it now . . . Sure." He held out the phone for Zack. "I assume you want managers for the budget, and recommendations from them on team members we can pull to help with the other problem?"

"Yes." Zack sat stunned. He could only watch as Nolan smiled and moved to his computer to tackle the day's disasters.

"Dude?" Max's voice echoed up from the cell. When Zack pressed it to his ear, he could hear him chuckling.

"Yup?"

"You need to seriously marry that man. He'll have you so organized you'll be running Compass, the gym, and probably my club within a year."

After everything that had happened, Zack doubted Nolan wanted anything else to do with him. "Say hi to your parents for me. I hope your mom is feeling better soon."

Zack's hand fell to his lap, the call ended, as he watched Nolan work. Had it only been a month since Nolan had come into his life? Watching Nolan's smooth, sure motions as he typed an email, a phone receiver pressed to his ear, was like watching a dancer move. This wasn't the same person who'd been freaking out in the bathroom before his interview. Or the same man he'd pressed against the wall at the gym.

A vulnerable Nolan had been a temptation he'd struggled to withstand. A confident Nolan was going to be the death of him.

Because Zack couldn't pretend that he was doing this new, stronger Nolan a favor by keeping his distance, keeping him safe from Zack's temper for fear of pushing him over the edge into panic. If there was no reason to keep him away, Zack might be tempted to let him in.

CHAPTER FIFTEEN

Nolan crossed the threshold of the Compass lobby and smiled as he placed a large coffee in front of Mindy, the security guard. "Good morning, my angel."

In the weeks after Ryan Cooper's attack on him and Zack, security had been paying extra attention to them to ensure nothing else happened. Nolan appreciated their assistance and wanted to make sure they knew it. Today, Zack had told him he didn't need him to come into the office until ten, which didn't make sense given how many things he could have done in those three hours. With nothing else to do, Nolan had spent a few minutes of his extra leisure time to swing by the coffee shop on his way into work.

Mindy had been working the security desk the day of his interview. It felt like a lifetime ago, when in fact it had only been a little over a month. Unlike on their first meeting, she smiled up at him. "You're the angel. How did you know I needed this?"

"Because it's a Tuesday, and nothing exciting ever happens on a Tuesday. Hence coffee." He put a full tray of additional coffees down in front of her. "For the boys."

"You don't need to suck up."

"Wouldn't dream of it. Just making sure that the people who keep me safe are taken care of. Have a good one."

He shouldn't be this happy, shouldn't whistle as he walked to the elevator, smiling at the people as he passed. The past few years had taught him to mistrust optimism. But it was hard to be gloomy when things were finally going his way. This morning before he'd left for work, Tina had told him she was finally moving to Vancouver.

"I'm sorry I was a jerk to you. I guess I was scared you wouldn't need me anymore. They said if I still want the position, they need me on a plane tomorrow. So . . . I guess this is it."

How could Tina think for even a moment that he wouldn't need her any longer? She was his big sister and best friend. She would always be the first person he'd call whenever something happened.

By the end of next week, the movers would have her things packed up and he'd be on his own. His heart had pounded in his chest the entire way to work, not from fear but from pure excitement. It was as though he'd finally earned back the right to resume his life as an adult. Tina was excited to be starting her new job, and his parents weren't calling daily worried about him. Even his job had smoothed out.

His days of dealing with soul-crushing anxiety every time he walked into the building were tapering off the longer he worked at Compass. Maybe, given enough time, he really would learn how to live with this the way his counselor had promised him he would.

No need to get ahead of things. There were still plenty of complications to deal with at work.

He'd spent most of the previous night thinking about what Zack had said to him. Remembering the way Zack had gently moved his hair away and looked without disgust at his scar. In those few minutes, something had shifted deep in his chest, as though a weight had moved from his soul. There hadn't been judgment in Zack's eyes, or anything that made Nolan feel like less of a man for the changes to his body.

For the first time since before the accident, he once again felt like a sexual being. Not only as an impulsive reaction, soon to be regretted, but with anticipation and intent.

It was wonderful.

Zack was in the office ahead of him. He dropped his things off on his desk and popped his head into Zack's office. "I thought you weren't coming in this morning? I was doing nothing when I could have been working."

"I'm technically not here." Zack smiled at him. "I'm doing departmental reviews and didn't want to be bothered."

"Oh. Sorry." He didn't think of himself as a pest. Maybe he'd have to work on that more—

"Not you. But if people see you sitting at the desk, then they come and chat, even if they think I'm gone. This way you got to sleep in, and I got to work uninterrupted." He leaned back in his seat. "Come in so someone doesn't spot you. Shut the door."

A shiver passed through Nolan. Things had calmed between them after Ms. Rollins had stormed into the office—the benefit of having a common foe. He'd kept his distance though, not sure exactly how he'd respond if things were to get intimate again. He wasn't uncomfortable or threatened. He was more concerned he'd be the one to take the next step, to react without thinking and kiss Zack. That would be a mistake, for all sorts of reasons.

It couldn't be excitement that spread through his body as he stepped inside and pressed the door shut. Nor was it anticipation as he cleared his throat and took a seat. It certainly wasn't arousal, because that would be inappropriate given what had passed between them. Honestly, he didn't know what he was feeling.

All of that. None of it. "What's up?" He should have noticed the moment he walked in, but now he was surprised when he saw how tired Zack looked. "How late were you working last night?"

Zack glanced at the clock. "I haven't gone home yet."

"Are you insane?" Nolan ignored his protests, grabbed his coffee mug, and left to refill it. On his way back he snagged an energy shot that he kept in his desk for emergencies. "Drink this. Tastes awful, but it'll give you a boost."

"Thanks." Zack's smile didn't make it to his eyes as he downed the energy shot. "Shit."

"Told you. The coffee makes a good chaser."

Zack breathed in the coffee fumes before taking a sip. "I'm glad you're here now."

"Couldn't get your own coffee?"

Zack scowled at him. "I need your help."

"Of course. With anything."

"I need your help to fire people."

Nolan shook his head. "That didn't work out so well for us last time."

"I know. And I appreciate that it's not an easy thing to do. But I've looked at the numbers, and I'm not sure I can cut costs any other way.

I don't have time to pore through and tweak every line item in this budget until I've freed up enough to keep everyone on. Not while also sorting through the mess with purchasing."

Their office was small, and it was Nolan's job to know what was going on in Zack's professional life. He'd heard the rumblings from Nancy as well, so it didn't come as that much of a surprise. That didn't make the idea any more welcome. "There's no other way?"

Zack ran his hand down his face. "That's what I've spent the last week looking at. Departmental budgets have come in, and I've been reviewing all capital expenditures. No one will admit to not needing something. I can throw it back to them and tell them to slash twenty percent of their nonpayroll expenditures, but I'm not sure I trust them, and I still wouldn't have time to review their reprioritized budgets."

"So you want my help to review everything?"

"No, I know this isn't your area of expertise. But you're an organizational master. You've found files and resources in the past month that I didn't know existed. If I'm going to find a way to save money, to save these jobs, then I'm going to need your help to dig."

"What about Chopra's proposal? Were you able to find any merit in that?"

"No. The prices were lower on hardware, but the technical specs were all wrong. Small changes to accommodate cost can have huge performance issues for our developers. Chopra should know that." Zack sighed and leaned back in his chair. "There has to be something I've missed."

In the month since he'd started the job, Nolan had experienced an array of Zack's moods. This was the first time he'd heard pleading. "Anything you need, I'm here to help."

Zack nodded, looking more than a little tired. "It's going to mean more late nights. Later than usual. I don't want your sister to be upset with me that I'm pushing you too much."

"Tina is moving to Vancouver. She flies out tomorrow, and her things will be following her by the end of the week. I'm officially on my own."

"Ah. That's good. I'm assuming that's good?"

Nolan smiled. "Yes, it's good."

"Well, if you feel up to it . . . Don't worry about transportation, I'll drive you home if need be. There will also be meals." Zack looked away and began to sort through the stack of file folders on his desk. "Why don't you get started with these? Read through and see if they're missing any supporting documentation."

Nolan's brain was still stuck on the whole *meals* thing. Their last shared meal—the sort-of-date leading to the revelation about Ringside—seemed like a lifetime ago. "I'll have a report by the end of the week."

"Thank you."

His feet carried him out of Zack's office as if by magic. It shouldn't strike him as that strange for Zack to offer to drive him home and feed him, especially if they were going to be working extra-long hours. It was the sign of a good employer, the sign of Zack being a good person, wanting to make sure he was looked after. There wasn't any reason to read more into it than that.

He picked up the phone and gave Tina a call. "Hey."

"Hey, you. What's up?"

"I just wanted to let you know that it looks like I'm going to have a late night."

"Later than normal? God, you'd think you staying until seven most nights would be good enough."

"Special circumstance. We have a major project to get done and it's all hands on deck. Sorry to miss your last night home, though."

"It's okay. I'll be back next weekend anyway to make sure I've gotten everything out of the place. Let me know if you need a ride."

"That's taken care of."

"The boss?"

"Yup."

He didn't need to see her face to know she was grinning. "Ah, it's one of *those* late work nights."

"Tina—"

"No, no, I get it. Just take it easy and make sure he walks you to the door when you're done."

"Ass."

"I love you too!"

He hung up and pulled open one of the files with a sigh. Ruler in hand, he began the arduous task of going line by line through the first of many budget sheets.

═ CHAPTER ═ SIXTEEN

Shortly after his conversation with Nolan, Zack had decided to take drastic measures: he'd pulled a team of managers and subject-matter experts together and sequestered them in a conference room with explicit instructions not to leave until they figured out how to cut costs across *all* their departments with minimal job reduction.

So far, they'd spent two days on the project, and Nolan had spent most of that time either laboring over budget and purchasing paperwork, or running between his office and the conference room. He'd made sure the team had all the supplies and information they needed, ensured food orders had arrived on time, and helped assistants with rescheduling canceled appointments. In his free time he'd coordinated with the contractor for Ringside.

The constant running around had his leg throbbing to the point where he was getting concerned about the amount of painkillers he'd taken. He couldn't remember being so exhausted since his first week of physio after the accident. Mentally and physically drained to the point that he'd gone past tired to delirious. Everything he saw was hilarious. He'd moved Ralph the spider from the farthest part of his desk to a prime location beside his keyboard. The fuzzy body was large and soft enough to act as a pillow, and if he could get over his irrational fear of the far-too-cute toy coming to life and eating his face, he might even use it as one.

No, no sleep yet.

Looking over at Zack's closed office door and wishing for it to open accomplished nothing. Zack had been on a call for over an hour, and there were no signs of it ending anytime soon. Nolan had been gauging the success of the call based on how frequently Zack's voice rose to a shout. It had been at least fifteen minutes since the last outburst, so things must finally be starting to go Zack's way.

He hated seeing Zack this stressed. Knowing now about Zack's long history with anger management, Nolan appreciated how hard he'd worked to keep his temper in check. Even his staff had noticed the change, and the management team had mentioned as much every time Nolan went to check on them.

Speaking of which . . .

It was almost 9 p.m., which meant the group looking at the invoices would be calling it a night soon. The report needed to be ready to present to Ms. Rollins in the morning; they'd assured Zack it would be finished before they left.

Nolan's back and leg screamed at him as he got to his feet and made the now familiar journey down the hall to the conference room. Plates, mugs, and half-eaten pizza were stacked on a trolley outside the room. The kitchen hadn't sent anyone to collect the dishes, which meant he'd have to take things down before he left for the night.

God, he was so done.

Ignoring the mess for the moment, he knocked on the door before stepping inside. The smell of alcohol, sweat, and stale pizza hit him within seconds. The group was gathered around a laptop laughing at something on the screen, their backs to the door. They hadn't noticed Nolan yet, which was probably the only reason he saw what they were watching.

Stretched out on a bed was a naked woman, who was being fucked by a man wearing a giant horse's head. Even if Nolan hadn't been gay, he didn't think he'd find anything the least bit arousing about the scene.

The man in the video whinnied loudly, and the guys watching it laughed again.

Nolan cleared his throat and waited for the group to turn around. "Mr. Anderson needs a status. But I assume you're done with the budget completely if you're watching porn and drinking at the office."

"Fuck off." Brian James, head of IT support, closed the laptop and took another drink from his mug. "We've been here for two days straight working our asses off. What Mr. Asshole wants us to do is fucking impossible."

The last thing they needed was for the team to revolt. Nolan swallowed his anger and consciously relaxed his shoulders before answering. "He's well aware of what's being asked of you. If there was any other way—"

Brian stood, pushing past the others to get right in Nolan's face. "I don't fucking see him here working."

Nolan tried not to breathe in too deeply. His heart pounded, and something tightened in the back of his throat. "He's in his office right now."

One of the others carefully slid Brian's mug from his hand before it could slop alcohol on a stack of documents, then patted him in a way that was clearly meant to be calming. "Back off, Brian. The lackey's just doing his job."

Brian shook off the hand on his shoulder and held his ground. "You're queer, right?"

"Brian man, come on—"

"Yes, I'm gay." Nolan had been lucky in his life to date: he hadn't run into many problems regarding his sexuality. Having three older, much larger brothers in high school prevented the bullying some of his friends had faced. But that didn't mean he hadn't been on the receiving end of his fair share of verbal abuse. It also didn't mean he couldn't defend himself. "Is that a problem?"

"Naw. You're too busy sucking your boss's cock to bother with mine."

For the first time in his life, Nolan wanted to hit someone. Anger warred with panic, making his head spin and his blood surge. "I think you've had too much to drink. Your friends better get you home before you do something stupid that gets you fired. Now."

After a few shared glances and nods of agreement, one of the group grabbed the laptop, a few backpacks, and a messenger bag, as another forced Brian out the door. The others followed suit, picking up belongings and vacating quickly. Before the last one left, he turned to Nolan. "We've been working our butts off and just needed to blow off some steam. We'd been asked to do the impossible."

"I know that. But you still can't watch porn on company equipment. And what you might not realize is that Mr. Anderson is dealing with this problem plus more."

"You're the only one who likes him. You know that, right? He's an ass who doesn't give a shit about anyone but himself." The guy shook his head, already walking toward the door again. "The report is done. We emailed it off five minutes ago." He disappeared around the doorframe, and a few seconds later Nolan heard the others laughing down the hall, and the faint *ding* of the elevator's arrival.

Nolan waited until he knew the group was gone, then turned off all the lights and fell into one of the abandoned conference room chairs. This was all too much for him, being the barrier between Zack and the rest of the world. With his eyes closed tight, he did his best to slow his breathing, and rubbed his thigh hard, willing the pain away.

How could people not see how much Zack cared about things, how much it killed him that he couldn't do enough for people? No one seemed to realize how big his heart was.

God, he couldn't sit in the dark sulking. There was too much to do, and whether Zack admitted it or not, he needed Nolan.

Zack's door was open when Nolan finally made his way back to the office. He walked in, not waiting to see if Zack was busy.

Zack looked up, dark smudges under his eyes. "Hey."

All thoughts of reports, delinquent staff, and construction jobs vanished. All Nolan saw was a man he'd come to respect, who he now considered a friend. A man he wanted nothing more than to kiss.

"Are you okay?" Zack pushed away from his desk.

Nolan couldn't speak. His throat was tight, unshed tears squeezing at his windpipe. He'd have to let his actions say what he felt. He closed the office door before moving around the desk. Zack still sat in his chair, but his eyes never left Nolan. It was a bit awkward, but Nolan turned Zack's seat so he could have better access, and dropped to his knees.

"What are you doing?" Zack's voice shook as he spoke.

"I was just accused of sucking your cock."

"What?" Zack was on his feet, ready to murder someone. "Who the hell said that to you?"

"It's irrelevant. What it did was get me thinking."

Zack swallowed and sat back down. "About what?"

"That I haven't actually seen your cock. Despite everything we've done, the time we've spent together, you've kept your distance from me." His fingers trembled as he fumbled with Zack's belt, though whether it was from exhaustion or anticipation, he didn't have a clue.

"Don't do this." Zack slid his hand across Nolan's, stilling his movements.

"You don't want me to do this?" He pressed Zack's erection with his fingers. "You seem to be on board."

"Who said you suck my cock?"

"Doesn't matter."

Zack reached up and took Nolan's face in his hands. "It matters."

For the first time since their moment at the gym, Nolan didn't fight the impulse to kiss him. Stretching his body, he pressed his mouth to Zack's and moaned as Zack immediately reciprocated. Hard muscles, firm hands, and the intoxicating scent that haunted Nolan's dreams surrounded him. Zack plundered his mouth, tongue exploring every inch of him. The intensity made Nolan's head spin, made him want more.

He pulled back, his eyes drifting closed. "I'm going to suck you now."

Zack ran his thumb along Nolan's bottom lip. "You don't have to do this."

"I want to. I've wanted to since I saw you in the bathroom that first day."

He didn't need to look to find Zack's belt and pull it open. His fingers still shook as he worked the zipper, but he knew now it was from excitement. The scent of arousal hit him as he reached into Zack's briefs and wrapped his fingers around his swollen shaft.

"Fuck, you're big." He stepped away from Zack to look down at his prize.

"I don't have a condom."

"Do I need one?"

"I don't have anything."

"I haven't had sex in years. I don't have anything." Nolan didn't wait; he pulled Zack's cock free of his pants. He stretched back the foreskin to reveal the red, swollen tip. "Fuck."

He teased the tip of Zack's cock, making sure to flick the head with the end of his tongue.

Zack groaned as he pushed his fingers into Nolan's hair. "Why didn't we do this the first time?"

Nolan licked a long trail up the length of Zack's shaft. "I didn't trust you then."

"But you do now?" Zack sucked a sharp breath in through his nose.

"Yup. Now, no more talking."

Together they worked Zack's pants down his hips so Nolan could push them to the floor. Fully exposed, Zack was completely at his mercy.

With his eyes closed, Nolan's other senses became heightened. Every sigh and moan that came from Zack embedded itself in his brain. The way the muscles in Zack's legs shook beneath his hands as he teased and caressed the skin. The warmth that rolled off Zack in waves every time Nolan swallowed down his cock.

God, Nolan wanted to be fucked by this man. He wanted to feel his body stretch around Zack, wanted to be held down by Zack's body and feel his orgasm rush through him. He dipped his head so he could suck on Zack's balls, run his tongue across the puckered skin and tease the jewel hidden beneath. The sac was tight, an indicator that Zack's release wouldn't be far off. As much as he wanted to be fucked, Nolan wanted to taste Zack's come even more.

Focusing his efforts, he worked Zack's cock, pumping and sucking until Zack's body shook beneath him.

"So fucking good." Zack thrust up into Nolan's mouth as he flexed his fingers against Nolan's jawline. "Gonna come."

Nolan groaned loudly around Zack's cock. Doubling down, he used his free hand to caress Zack's balls, rub his taint and lower until he rimmed his asshole with one fingertip. The teasing was enough. Zack held Nolan's head still while he increased his thrusts. The head of his cock threatened to brush the back of Nolan's throat, forcing him to relax his muscles, to accept everything Zack gave him.

The first spurt of hot come splashed across his tongue, and Nolan did his best to swallow it down. Zack moaned; his fingers squeezed Nolan's head, pulled his hair as he came with jerky thrusts. His come was bitter in Nolan's mouth; it didn't matter.

He wasn't sure if Zack had finished or not, because the next thing Nolan knew he was being tugged to his feet and manhandled to lie on Zack's desk. "I want you."

"Me too."

Zack made short work of his belt and zipper. He yanked Nolan's pants down, hesitating only when Nolan stiffened. "What?"

Jesus, he couldn't freak out now, not when several of his more erotic fantasies were about to come to life. But the throbbing in his leg was enough of a reminder about his scars, about the ugliness that covered his thigh. Zack didn't know what he was getting himself into, and Nolan didn't have a clue how he'd react.

"I have scars. They're not pretty."

Zack frowned. "Am I hurting you?"

"No."

"Do you want me to stop?"

"Fuck no."

"Then I don't care about the scars." He leaned in and kissed Nolan hard. "Now relax and enjoy this."

Zack slipped off Nolan's shoes so he could free his legs from his pants. The cool office air sent a chill through him as he lost the only thing hiding his scars from Zack. He held his breath as Zack reached out and ran a finger across the worst of the wounds on his leg. "Shit."

The trail of damage led from midthigh to his stomach. Zack pushed his shirt out of the way, following the injury as much as he could. "How did you walk away from that?"

I didn't walk, I was airlifted. "Luck."

If what he saw bothered him, Zack said nothing. He instead slipped his fingers into the band of Nolan's briefs and pulled them down, until Nolan was left wearing only his shirt. "I won't fuck you without a condom. I won't do that to you."

Nolan shuddered. "I trust you."

"No. The first time I push into you, I'll do it right. But I will do this."

He forced Nolan's legs apart, and ran his hands up Nolan's thighs until he bracketed his hard cock. "I'm going to jerk you off."

With his hand around Nolan's shaft, Zack moved between his knees, which let Nolan wrap his legs around Zack's waist. Zack was still hard, and he pressed his cock against Nolan's ass cheeks.

They were so close, nearly to the place where Nolan desperately wanted to be. Zack moved his hips in time with the stroking of Nolan's cock. While he might not be inside him, he moved in such a way that Zack's cock, still slick from Nolan's saliva, rubbed between Nolan's cheeks, teasing his asshole and leaving nothing to the imagination.

Every time he and Zack were alone, Nolan's body responded. He'd been walking around the office half-hard for so long his world had dissolved into a near-constant state of arousal. But with Zack's hands finally on him, the barriers were gone. They were both free to see where they could take each other.

Zack's thrusts increased in tempo as he squeezed his hand around Nolan's cock. "Stay with me. Don't let that mind of yours wander."

Nolan chuckled, then a gasp escaped him as Zack's fingers tightened again. "Not going anywhere."

"Tell me what you want. What you've been thinking about."

"You." Forcing his eyes open, he made sure to look directly at Zack. "I wish we were in a bed. That we had lube and time and that you'd stretch me open with your fingers just enough so I could take that big cock of yours into me. I want you to fill me and press me down. I want to taste your sweat like I've swallowed your come."

The longer he spoke, the closer to orgasm he got. Perspiration had broken out across his body, causing his ass and the small of his back to slide across the desk.

Zack's pupils dilated and his mouth fell open. "Dirty mouth."

"Yeah."

Zack lowered his voice as he leaned forward. "I want to hear you scream my name. I want to fuck you so hard you feel me for days after. I want you to get fucking hard every time you think about me."

The tip of Zack's cock pressed against his asshole, and for a second, Nolan thought he was going to break his promise and take him after all. That was enough to push him over the edge. Nolan sucked a breath through his nose and clamped his mouth shut, forcing back the scream he so desperately wanted to unleash.

Come shot from him to land across his shirt, his stomach, and Zack's hand. The waves of his orgasm rolled through him over and over until he was aware of nothing but the all-consuming pleasure.

Finally, everything stopped. Pleasure still clung to his body, even as Zack carefully pulled away and arranged Nolan's legs so his feet rested on Zack's chair. "Don't move."

"Couldn't if I wanted to."

Zack got dressed and disappeared, only to return with a damp paper towel from the kitchen. "Best I can offer."

"I'll be sure to put some wet wipes in the cupboard if there's going to be a repeat performance."

Zack reached down and used Nolan's tie to gently tug him into a seated position. "The next time this happens will be in a bed. The next time will involve condoms and fucking and screaming."

There was no mistaking the lust in Zack's voice, no doubt about how serious he was with his prediction.

"So there will be a next time?" Nolan's voice was far quieter than he would have liked.

Zack pulled Nolan closer and bit down on his chin. "Yes."

"What about you being my boss?"

"Do you care?"

"No."

"Then I don't either."

It was a lie, but one Nolan would happily accept. "When?"

"Once this mess is done, once we have time to breathe. I'm going to bring you home and fuck you until you beg me to stop."

Nolan swallowed hard. "I can't wait."

Even though waiting was exactly what they had to do.

=CHAPTER=
SEVENTEEN

Zack was late. It hadn't been intentional, but with all the long nights and early mornings he'd put in this week, he'd been exhausted and slept through his alarm. Of all the days, this was the wrong one not to be on his A game.

He'd spent the better part of yesterday with the budget team, ironing out the remaining details. It wasn't pretty, and no one had been happy about the reductions in their discretionary budgets, but the alternative was the loss of five positions across three teams. No one wanted that. The day had been more emotionally draining than he'd realized.

All that remained was for Zack to have his meeting with Samantha later this afternoon and report on his findings.

He'd barely made it into the building's lobby when Nolan came bounding out of the elevator. "Oh, perfect timing."

"I'm late."

"Not at all." He hooked his arm through Zack's and spun him around. "We have a meeting."

"Where?"

"The special project you put me in charge of."

He must have really been tired, because it took Zack more than a few seconds to realize what Nolan meant. Ringside. "What's going on?"

"All good. We can walk."

He groaned, but let himself be pulled along. "We don't really have time for this."

"You absolutely do. Your meeting with Ms. Rollins got moved to Monday—"

"*What?*"

"—so you have breathing room." Nolan cringed, but didn't stop moving. "I knew you'd be pissed."

"Damn right I'm pissed. We killed ourselves for her, and she's not even here to get what she demanded out of us."

Nolan gave his arm a quick squeeze before letting it go. "I know. But I have something you need to see that will change your mood. Okay?"

Nothing about this entire situation was *okay*. "I have nothing else to do, apparently. Fine."

The streets were busy with morning commuters, shoppers, and people going about their day. By the time they reached the gym, Zack was more than ready to be done with all of them. "Okay, what was so important?"

He should have known something big was up simply from the look of excitement on Nolan's face. The moment they stepped through the doors, the sounds of people working overwhelmed him.

Gone was the stench of mold and grime that used to hit him whenever he walked into the old building; in its place were the smell of cleaning supplies and the sounds of young voices.

"What the hell's going on?"

Nolan's grin brightened. "With you so busy the past week, I had a bit of time to work out the details with the contractor. We're going to have him and the students every day for the next three weeks. When he found out what you were planning to do with the place, the youth programs, he was able to get some of his buddies on board as well. We still have to pay them for labor, but it's cheap and they're getting us all the materials at barely above cost."

Zack didn't know what to say. He'd dreamed for so long about finally making some headway with this project, but he had never been able to make any progress. It had taken Nolan only a week to accomplish more than what Zack and Max together had done in six months.

"I thought there was paperwork? Max said there was a shit-ton and it would take weeks."

"Well, there is. I talked to the school, found out what we can and can't do, what we need permission for, etc." Nolan shrugged.

"Still some things to finalize. Today was supposed to simply be a scouting session. But when they got here and saw the state of the place, they bought some cleaning supplies and got to work."

"I could kiss you."

The blush that exploded across Nolan's cheeks was stunning. "Please don't. Until later, I mean."

Their moment of privacy evaporated when the contractor came over and introduced himself. Zack grilled him on a number of points before talking to some of the students. It seemed they were all interested in taking some lessons once the youth program was up and running. He answered as many questions as he could, all the while completely aware of Nolan. Like he normally did, Nolan had slid into the background, letting Zack take center stage.

Before he knew it, the boys went back to work, and he and Nolan were on their way to the office.

"Max will be blown away by what you've managed to do in such a short time. If you're not careful, he'll be after you to come run Frantic for him."

"I have a boss, thanks."

Zack stopped and took Nolan by the arm. "I'm more than that."

"What?"

God, he was too cute when he was surprised. "I'd like to think I'm your friend."

Nolan's blush returned. "Of course."

"And your lover."

It was so easy to say the words, even standing in the middle of a crowded street. Here they were anonymous, two men in a city of millions. Two lonely, horny men who'd drifted along in their lives until they'd crashed together. Zack knew as soon as they returned to work they'd fall into their normal roles, and Nolan would fade into the background, doing all the dirty work that no one else would.

Nolan cared so deeply. He'd been hurt, yet somehow managed to continue helping others. For one day, Zack wanted to enjoy that man, to be with Nolan and not his assistant. He didn't want clandestine sexual moments; he wanted a day to appreciate the company of a man he'd grown to admire and care for.

"Is everything ready for Monday's meeting with Samantha?"

"As ready as it can be. We now have three extra days to confirm the details, but everything was in your inbox this morning when I arrived."

"Good. Can the guys lock up the gym when they're done?"

Nolan gaped at him before nodding. "Of course. I had to give them a key and the code—"

"Let's go." Zack didn't give him time to react; he tugged Nolan along with him when he didn't immediately move.

"Where . . . What are . . . Hey!"

"Keep walking. We're going for breakfast."

Nolan stumbled briefly before getting his footing and falling into step beside him. Zack held on to his hand to ensure he wouldn't take off.

For his part, Nolan didn't try to pull away. "You do realize that it's almost noon."

"Brunch, then. I'm hungry and tired and want to enjoy your company."

Zack had worked for years trying to not be the man who gave in to every impulse, whether it was his anger, lust, or any other emotion. He failed some days, but he'd learned to keep moving forward after the occasional slip. He could allow himself this indulgence. Giving in to this urge to be with Nolan, to keep him all to himself for a few hours, was something that couldn't have a downside.

Since he was acting on impulse, there was no reason not to throw all caution to the wind. Instead of going to a swanky restaurant, he marched them over to a street vendor. "Sausage with kraut, and a pretzel. What do you want?"

"Ah, same. I guess." Nolan was staring at him, no doubt trying to determine whether he'd had a nervous breakdown.

"I'm fine."

"If you say so."

It was probably for the best that Nolan didn't realize how close Zack was to kissing him right then. How much he wanted to take him home and spend the next several hours stripping him bare to fuck him into the mattress.

Now that he thought about it . . .

He waited until the vendor handed over their food. Then he paid with the twenty he kept in his wallet for emergencies and led Nolan to the street to flag down a cab.

"Where are you taking me now?" Nolan followed the question with a huge bite of his sausage. When he licked his lips, removing some of the greasy residue from his skin, Zack knew he wasn't going to make it all the way to a private place before giving in to his next impulse.

Grabbing Nolan by the tie, he pulled him in for a hard kiss, drawing it out just long enough to lick some of the grease for himself. "Home. Now."

He could have walked them back to the office so he could get his car and drive them to his condo, but that would have wasted precious time. Every minute they took to get back to his place was a minute he couldn't take to seduce Nolan properly.

If Nolan had any issues with the plan, he didn't voice them. When a cab finally stopped for them, they fell into the back, happily crowding one another. Zack held himself in check for the entire ride, eating his breakfast without really tasting it. The food had quickly become irrelevant; it was simply another thing in the way, delaying the acquisition of his prize.

The ride took too long. Paying the cabbie took too long. The elevator took too long and was also far too crowded for his liking. When they finally reached his floor, Zack grabbed Nolan's arm and tugged him along once again.

Nolan did nothing to stop Zack, but when they reached his condo door and Zack threw it open, Nolan didn't move immediately from the hall to follow him inside.

Zack finally stopped and really looked at him. "Are you okay?"

Nolan swallowed and looked down the hall toward the elevator. "Yup."

Fuck, he'd screwed up again. "You don't have to come in. I want you to. I want to get you naked on my bed. I want to lick and touch every inch of you. But if you don't want the same, you can say no. You can walk away and nothing will change."

"If I come in, everything will change." Nolan shook his head. "I'm not sure I'm ready for that."

"How so? How could you being here, letting me treat you with the respect you deserve, be wrong in any way?"

Nolan chuckled. "Is this about me? You've barely looked at me since the gym. Just dragged me along behind you all the way here."

"Of course it's about you." Zack held his arms open and tried to choose his words carefully, terrified that he'd mess this up, say the wrong thing, and lose his chance forever. "I . . . I know my faults. I know what others think of me, and until recently, I'd accepted that I was the office villain. My temper was my weakness, and no matter how much I tried to shove it deep down, I was destined to fail. It wasn't until you showed up in my life that I found a way to keep things together. Your presence, you simply being near me has changed me, my perception of things."

Nolan didn't say anything, but Zack could see unshed tears building in his eyes.

"I know that sounds like it's about me. I'm not saying it well. You . . . you've been through so much in the past few years. You've had to rebuild your life, changing the things that made you who you were. It didn't stop you. I don't think I'd have been able to rebuild my life the way you've had to, and still stay caring of others. It's . . . inspiring. You make me want to be better. But I'm not good at saying it. If you come in, I can *show* you what I think of you, how much I've come to respect you. How much I want to make love to you."

Nolan choked out a half sob, half laugh. "You suck at seduction."

"I know." He held out his hand. "I've always been a man of action."

It took a moment, but Nolan finally slipped his hand into Zack's. "Okay, then."

Nolan's heart pounded so hard in his chest he was terrified he'd have a heart attack before he saw this—whatever this was with Zack—through to its conclusion. Sex? Yeah, they were totally going to have proper naked sex, possibly even in a bed. If it were simply that, Nolan knew he wouldn't be freaking out the way he currently was.

Nolan hadn't felt so overwhelmed since his last visit to Frantic, and that hadn't ended the way he'd hoped. If he wanted to avoid the descent into a full-blown panic attack, then he needed to catch his breath and go through his anxiety-reduction techniques.

If Zack was bothered by his damp hands, he didn't say anything. Zack led him into the living room; big windows flanked by long gray curtains filled the far wall. Light spilled across the hardwood floor, creating beautiful patterns while bits of dust sparkled in the beams. Aside from that, the condo was clean and hardly looked lived in. Nolan turned around and took in as much as he could. There was a lingering scent of furniture polish or some other cleaning supply. Having seen how messy Zack's office got, Nolan had no doubt he paid for a cleaning service here.

There wasn't a lot of personality, nothing that screamed out *Zack Anderson lives here, see!* But the generic look of the space had a calming effect on Nolan; it seemed like neutral territory. He felt some tension drain from his shoulders, and realized his breathing had already slowed down. His heart still raced, but not from panic.

The honk of cars on the streets below easily reached him, as did the click and whir of the fridge compressor coming on.

He felt Zack move behind him, noted the smell of his aftershave and the lingering scent of the sausage they'd eaten.

"Let me take your coat."

Warm hands slid Nolan's suit coat from his shoulders, fingers grazing his arms as Zack freed him from the material. The heat that had encased him since they'd climbed into the cab dissipated, leaving his nipples hard from the change. Hot breath tickled the back of his neck, making it nearly impossible for him to concentrate on anything beyond Zack.

He was only vaguely aware of Zack tossing the jacket somewhere behind them. He was more focused on the press of Zack's body against his back, the gentle caress of fingertips along his sides, and the subtle thrust of a hard cock against his ass.

"Can I get you anything?" Zack's voice was a rumble beside his ear. His fingers ghosted to Nolan's stomach to tease the skin hiding beneath his shirt. "A drink?"

"No."

Zack moved both hands to Nolan's waistband. "Do you need me to stop?"

"God, no." He didn't know what might happen beyond this day, past this moment. He wasn't willing to stop or even pause, for fear that they'd never have another chance.

Sure fingers began to work the front of his pants open. Hands brushed across the fabric of his briefs, sending chills through Nolan and making his cock impossibly hard. Unlike their previous times together, there was no sense of urgency or danger. There was no risk of them getting caught, or running out of time.

His anxiety didn't threaten to rear up and ruin what could possibly be the best moment of his recent life. He gave himself permission to relax and simply be with Zack, enjoy their stolen time together in the middle of the day. He leaned against Zack's chest and let his head fall back until it rested on Zack's shoulder.

A soft groan was punctuated by a roll of Zack's hips. "I haven't been able to get you out of my head. I've jerked off nightly remembering what we've done together. I want more. Always more."

Briefly, Nolan thought he might pass out. No one had ever said these things to him before, had wanted him for anything more than a few dates. He felt special, and the fact that these words were being spoken by a man like Zack made it all the more special.

Fingers at his throat, working his tie open, had Nolan swallowing hard. When Zack began to work open his shirt buttons, he held his breath and tried to memorize each brush against his throat.

Zack took his time, teasing Nolan's chest as he nipped and licked at his neck. His cock stiffened more at the sound of Zack's clothing against his, the occasional catch of Zack's breath, the press of Zack's erection against his ass.

Shit, this was really going to happen.

"What do you like? What do you want?" Zack rubbed his thumb across Nolan's nipple. "Do you want me to tease you?"

He chuckled. "I think any teasing you'd do is likely to kill me."

"That sounds like a challenge."

"It so wasn't."

"Fairly certain it was." Zack nipped the side of his neck. "A chance to see if I can make my resourceful, sexy assistant come apart before I fuck him senseless. That's a challenge I'll happily take."

God, he was so screwed.

Still pressed against his back, Zack directed him toward a hallway. "Bedroom is that way."

A bed was a good idea. "That's the best plan you've had all week." Nolan reached back awkwardly and squeezed Zack's ass.

If Zack had another smart-ass comeback, he didn't manage to get it out before he moaned against Nolan. The gentle prodding to move quickly became commanding shoves. There was only so much either of them could take, and apparently Zack was close to his limit.

Which was a good thing because Nolan didn't know how long he'd last with all of this stimulation.

The walk to Zack's bedroom was made challenging by his loosened pants. They shuffled along as they stole kisses and touches until Zack pushed open the bedroom door. This was the one room Nolan had assumed would contain something of Zack, but it was much the same as the rest of his place: neat and slightly impersonal. Maybe he didn't spend much time here and simply never got around to decorating it to his liking. Still, something about it broke Nolan's heart.

"What is going on in that brain of yours?" Zack turned him around and looked right into his eyes. "You stiffened up. Do you want me to stop?"

"No!" He laughed and shook his head. "Not at all. I was surprised at how . . . how . . ." He waved his hand around the room. "Doesn't scream *Zack*."

Zack responded with an eye roll and shoved him onto the bed. "Please criticize my home *after* sex. I promise you'll see it in a better light when we're done." He started on his clothing, holding Nolan's gaze as he did.

There was no way Nolan could have looked away, even if he'd wanted to.

As far as he was concerned, there was nothing more intimate than watching a man get undressed. It didn't matter if they were putting on a show or not; for Nolan, the act of stripping off the layers, leaving no barriers between them, showed a level of trust he cherished. Zack, more than any other person he knew, constantly lived behind a wall. He'd caught glimpses of the man hidden beneath the fortifications in their previous stolen moments. But here and now, watching Zack undo each button as he revealed inch after inch of his firm chest, Nolan knew everything would be on display.

The soft *whoosh* of cotton falling to the floor registered somewhere in Nolan's head, but most of his attention was trained on his first sight of a half-naked Zack. Dark chest hair covered firm pecs, trailing down to dust a six-pack. Shit, Nolan had known Zack was fit, had felt as much before, but sitting in front of him—eyes to abs—was a nearly religious experience.

The vision also severely contrasted with Nolan's broken body.

"I've never had sex with someone as hot as you." Nolan hesitated, but finally reached out and trailed his fingers across Zack's stomach. "How are you even real?"

"I'm very real and far from perfect." Zack cupped Nolan's cheek, caressing the skin with his thumb. "You of all people should know that."

Turning his face into Zack's hand, Nolan kissed his palm. "I think we're talking too much."

"I think you're right." Zack gently pushed Nolan's shoulders until he was lying on his back. "Now, where was I?"

Nolan grinned. "Getting naked?"

"You first."

His pants were already undone, so when Zack reached down to slide them off his legs, there was little he could do to slow the process. It didn't matter that Zack had already seen his scars; the moment the cool air brushed across the exposed skin, Nolan's heart pounded and his throat tightened.

Zack's gaze raked Nolan's body, but he didn't come any closer. "Are you okay?"

Nolan turned his head and inhaled. Zack's scent clung to the duvet. "Yeah."

The weight of Zack sitting on the bed jostled him. The touch of fingers on his thigh made his breath catch.

Zack rested his fingertips along one ridged line of scar tissue. "This really bothers you? What it looks like, I mean?"

"I don't understand how it doesn't bother you." When Nolan looked into Zack's eyes, it surprised him to see no revulsion. "It's horrid."

He wasn't sure what he was expecting, but it certainly wasn't Zack shifting position so his face hovered above Nolan's leg, nor the gentle kiss Zack placed on the worst of the damage. Nolan's cock—already hard—twitched at the contact. God, it would have been even better if Zack had taken his briefs off too. The touch of Zack's wet tongue on his gnarled skin ripped a moan from him.

"It's not horrid. Our bodies tell a story of who we are and what we've done." He continued to kiss up to the band of Nolan's briefs. "You've been through so much. That's what I see."

When Zack hooked his fingers around the elastic of Nolan's briefs and looked up into his eyes, Nolan's world came to a screeching halt. For the first time he really saw Zack, the man behind the mask, the person hiding behind the persona who fought the world. He saw the man who struggled with his emotions, who wanted more and better from his life, but didn't know how to get it.

Nolan saw passion, determination, and lust—and it was all directed at him. "Fuck."

Zack grinned. "I plan to."

The remaining playfulness evaporated as Zack slid Nolan's briefs down; the shock of air on his heated cock pulled another moan from him. It was clear that Zack had no intention of wooing him, of gently seducing him. No, with a gleam in his eyes, he leaned over and sucked on the tip of Nolan's cock. Nolan's fingers curled, squeezing the comforter in a vain attempt to keep from moving. Zack's mouth worked him hard and fast, his tongue explored every inch of skin while his hands caressed Nolan's scars.

All of Nolan's fears about being with a lover and having them be repulsed by what they saw fell away. It didn't matter to Zack, so there was no reason why it should matter to Nolan. He let his body relax and his mind drift. It was so easy to simply *be*, to feel pleasure in a way he hadn't experienced in years.

"Yeah, that's it." Zack nipped the inside of his thigh. "Spread your legs for me."

Jesus, he's going to kill me. Not that he was about to stop Zack from doing what he wanted. *Fuck that.* Nolan let his legs fall open, exposing himself to Zack and his roaming hands.

"You're so fucking hot." Zack pulled back and went to work undressing. "I want to take you like that, on your back so I can see your face."

Nolan groaned. "Yes."

The next few minutes became a blur of movement, touching, the occasional frantic kiss. Yes, this was finally happening. He was ready and wanted nothing more than to feel Zack stretch him wide. The moment Zack kicked his own pants and briefs free and went in search of a condom in his nightstand drawer, Nolan's arousal spiked. God, he wasn't going to last long when they finally got around to the whole sex thing.

Zack rolled the condom on and climbed back on the bed, stretching out beside him. "You're flushed."

"I'm fucking horny." His cock twitched to drive the point home.

Zack chuckled and ran a finger up the length of his shaft. "I think we need to slow things down a bit."

"No. No slowing down." He reached over and pulled Zack's head down for a kiss. "Fuck me."

"I will. In time."

Nolan's frustration tapered off as Zack continued the kiss, soft and steady. Stubble scratched his face as Zack deepened their contact. Zack leaned over him, half covering his body, cupping his face with large, warm hands. His brain lost the ability to form complete thoughts as his body became a live wire, sparking from every point of contact. The energy became warmth that filled every inch of his body. He'd heard people say that during sex they became one with their partner, that they underwent some sort of emotional merging. He'd always chalked that up to silly romanticizing . . . God, what an idiot he'd been.

When Zack broke the kiss and rubbed his nose against Nolan's, the sudden rush of unexpected affection made it hard to breathe. How could one man become so utterly vital to his life, to his happiness, without his even realizing?

He swallowed down the hard lump in his throat. "Please."

Zack caressed his cheek, frowning. "You okay?"

"Please." He opened his legs again. "Please."

Zack must have understood exactly what Nolan wanted. Without another word, he grabbed the bottle of lube from where he'd tossed it on the bed and squirted a generous amount on his fingers. Holding eye contact, he pressed a single finger into Nolan's ass, pumping slowly enough to relax the muscles before adding a second.

"You're so tight." Zack placed a kiss to his chest.

"I'm ready." To underline his point, Nolan thrust down on Zack's fingers.

Zack's eyes rolled up into his head. "You're going to kill me." Apparently, he was all for that death, because he moved between Nolan's legs and pushed his knees up and wide, exposing his hole.

Nolan did his best to relax his body, but the mix of excitement, adrenaline, and lust was too much for him to fight. The first kiss of cock to hole pulled a sigh from him, his body shaking from anticipation. Zack slid his hands along the insides of Nolan's thighs as he steadily inched forward. The stretch of muscles, the intimacy of the caress, the smell of Zack so present and all-encompassing made Nolan love drunk.

The further in Zack pressed, the louder his moans grew. "So. Tight."

Nolan's voice had fled, leaving his body the only method of communication. He bucked his hips, encouraging Zack on until he was finally balls-deep inside him. They stayed that way for a moment, eyes locked and bodies entwined. Nolan could barely breathe, was terrified to move in case he came. God, he couldn't believe this was happening.

The muscles in Zack's jaw twitched, and his fingers flexed around Nolan's legs. That was the only warning he gave before he set a steady pace. Nolan's cock lay heavy and hard against his stomach, leaking and begging to be touched. Zack's gaze traveled down and locked on to it. Nolan knew if either of them touched it, the end would come rapidly. Still, with Zack's gaze where it was, he couldn't stop from wanting to give him everything.

Keeping his eyes on Zack, Nolan reached down and began to fist his shaft, stroking a counter-rhythm to Zack's thrusts. "Not gonna last long."

"Jesus." Zack faltered briefly before he slammed into Nolan. "Fuck."

The note of awe in Zack's voice caught him off guard. Nolan's hand flew over his cock as he felt his balls tighten, and he knew the end was approaching hard and fast. The first spurts of come shot across his stomach before his brain registered the initial burst of pleasure. Then every muscle tightened as wave after wave of orgasm rolled through him. It wasn't enough, the sensation lacked something. Blindly, he reached up for Zack and pulled gently until he moved. "Please."

With come now sliding between their bodies, Zack pressed his face to Nolan's neck and moaned against him. Yes, that was what he'd needed, the feel of another person's sweat against his skin. The smell of a man who wanted him for all the right reasons. The sounds of desire and sex against his ear, loud enough to rattle around his brain for the rest of his life.

Zack's body tensed, his teeth scraped Nolan's shoulder. Staccato thrusts pushed Nolan down into the mattress; firm muscles against his chest stole the air from his lungs. Zack shuddered, and nearly as quickly as everything had begun, it came crashing to a halt.

Once Nolan caught his breath, he ran his fingers back and forth along the planes of Zack's shoulders. He made patterns in the sweat, dancing his fingertips across slick skin. He thought Zack might have drifted off to sleep. It wasn't until the gentle kiss just below his ear that he realized Zack had been as settled into the moment as Nolan.

"Do you need me to move?" Zack pressed his nose further against him. "Am I hurting you?"

"I'm good." For the first time in a very long time, he really was. A blanket of peace had slipped over him, and he knew that despite everything that had changed in his life, he would push on and would be okay.

They stayed there entwined so long that Nolan started to nap; he protested when Zack eventually slipped from his body. It earned him a nip to the end of his nose.

"Stop it. I need to get us cleaned up."

"Overrated." He rolled to his side and did his best to ignore the pain in his leg.

"You won't say that when you're picking dried come out of your stomach hair."

"True."

In the past, the few necessary minutes of cleanup had always felt awkward to Nolan. In a way, it was far more intimate than the sex itself. What they did and how they did it said a lot about his partners and what they thought about him. Gentle or efficient; playful or serious. He watched Zack pad to the bathroom, stripping the condom as he went, his tight ass a beacon in the light.

Zack grabbed a clean cloth from beneath the counter and dampened it. Nolan could see part of his face in the bathroom mirror; a smile played on his lips before he spoke, not glancing up from his task at the sink.

"I don't know about you, but I'm hungry again. Want to get something to eat? Real food this time."

"Sure."

Nolan couldn't look away as Zack returned, leaned down, and kissed him. He held his breath when Zack pressed the cloth to his stomach and began to clean up the come.

After a few minutes of careful but silent attention to Nolan's hygiene, Zack passed the damp cloth off. "You rest for a few minutes while I check my email. Need to make sure the world isn't falling apart while we're gone."

In a blink, Nolan was alone.

He stretched his muscles, actually enjoying the slight discomfort from where Zack had pounded him moments ago. It seemed less important than the vague anxiety starting to swirl around in his brain. Sure, his body was sated, but he couldn't help but be disappointed at Zack's sudden disappearance. It was reasonable for Zack to check in, and really to be expected given the time of day and how long they'd been incommunicado. Still, when Zack didn't return within the specified few minutes, Nolan worried that Zack had forgotten about him. A short time after that, when Zack still didn't return, Nolan's concern turned from self-indulgent to genuine. Had something happened?

"You coming back?"

Silence was the only response. *That wasn't right.* Not bothering to grab his clothing, he followed Zack's path until he came to the living room. Zack stood in the middle of the room, naked and looking down at his phone.

"Hey..." Nolan walked over, wanting to touch Zack, but not sure if he should. "Everything okay?"

"No. Everything is not okay."

It was only then that Nolan noticed the death grip Zack had on the phone. "What's going on?"

"Samantha is." Zack threw the phone across the room, smashing it against the wall.

"Shit, calm down." Nolan stepped back, suddenly uncertain about what might happen next. He'd forgotten so quickly how volatile Zack could be, and how those mood swings affected him.

"I can't fucking calm down. That bitch!" Zack marched over to the window, his arms bent up so the insides of his elbows pressed to his ears.

The peace was gone, and in its stead was panic. But Nolan forced himself to exhale, and focused on what was within his ability to control: he needed more information. "Tell me. I can't help you if I don't know what's going on."

"All of our work, everything. None of it mattered."

The hell? "What do you mean?"

When Zack turned to face Nolan, there was nothing hiding the rage he clearly felt. "She announced layoffs. She'd been planning it all along."

CHAPTER EIGHTEEN

Zack wasn't used to being ignored, not even by his boss. So the fact that he'd been standing outside of Samantha's office for the better part of forty-five minutes Monday morning had done nothing but allow his anger to grow into a raging beast. He'd given up sitting ten minutes earlier; it was either pace around the waiting room and glare at Samantha's assistant, or run the risk of yelling at the poor woman who'd done nothing wrong.

Nolan would have his head on a pike if he did that.

God, Nolan. He hadn't wanted to leave him and their escape on Friday, but they'd had no choice but to return to the office. Not that it had done Zack any good. Samantha hadn't been around—no doubt she'd been hiding out, anticipating how he'd react when he got the news. Zack had sent Nolan away, amidst a flurry of arguments that he had nothing to do at home and was more than happy to stay and help all weekend. For a moment, Zack had been tempted to take him up on the offer, but there was nothing they realistically could have done, so they left.

This morning, he needed his anger to push him forward, to fuel his drive and ensure that this current bullshit would be dealt with. Get rid of ten percent of his team? Was Samantha *insane*? Not only was it unnecessary, putting needless hardship on the impacted employees, it would send ripples throughout the whole company. Morale and loyalty would crater, and everybody would start polishing their résumés and sniffing around for escape routes.

Samantha's voice echoed through her closed door a moment before the handle turned. Zack ignored the assistant and got in the way the second the door opened. Nancy from HR was on the other side, looking more than a little pale. No doubt she'd been given a horrible assignment.

"Mr. Anderson." Nancy glanced behind her to where Samantha stood glaring, before sliding past him.

Samantha might be many things, but easily intimidated wasn't one of them. Holding Zack's gaze for several long moments, she finally sighed. "Carm, can you please hold my calls?"

"Yes, Ms. Rollins."

"Come in, Zack."

He had to bite his tongue to keep from saying something that would get him immediately fired. It was Nolan's advice he heard in his head: *"Keep it simple and ask your questions, don't get mad and it'll all be fine."*

He crossed his arms and stared down at Samantha when she took her seat behind her desk. "What the fuck is going on?"

"And good morning to you too." She laced her fingers together and gave her head a shake. "I'd ask what you'd like to discuss, but I don't need to."

"What was the point of me putting my staff through hell, making them spend nights for a week to cut expenditures so we could save jobs, when you never had any intention of saving them *in the first place?*" His voice had grown to a roar that left his body shaking.

No, he couldn't lose his shit. It would accomplish nothing and would only serve to get him in trouble. Pulling in a long, slow breath, he counted to ten in his head. God, it was annoying that the voice he heard counting was Nolan's.

Clearing his throat, he forced his arms to his sides. "Sorry, let's start again."

"Probably for the best." Samantha leaned back, but gave no indication of how she was feeling.

"Good morning, Ms. Rollins. I received your email about the layoffs. I was hoping we could discuss the particulars." *You coldhearted backstabber.*

"Have a seat, though there's really only so much we can change."

Fine. He'd handled situations and people as hard-nosed as Samantha before; he could do it now. Taking the guest seat, he spread his legs wide and lowered his chin to look directly at her. "Why is this happening?"

Samantha tapped the edge of her desk with her finger, a move she did when she was making a decision. "The board had a meeting. We're going to be taking Compass public in the next six months."

"That's good. I'm surprised they hadn't made that decision before now."

"They didn't because of what needed to happen first. The company needs to get lean. We need to streamline processes, costs, get the books shining so when we hit the market we're poised to launch straight up."

It made sense, and having this bit of information helped slot a lot of seemingly left-field requests from the past year into place. They wanted to clean house before their every move fell under investors' microscopes. He bit back his first impulse—to pound a fist on the desk and demand to know why he hadn't been looped in to begin with—and bought himself some time to think instead. "Okay. I see. So, the extra budget request, the layoffs . . ."

Samantha nodded. "All preparation. The board set a date, and we have to meet it, no matter what."

A bubble of rage made it to the surface. "This is *wrong*. There must be another way to keep staff and still ensure the books are ready for a public offering."

"Do you think we're doing this for the hell of it? The severance packages will be there—it's a financial weight that we're not taking on lightly. We've cut and trimmed where we could, but this is more than just bookkeeping. It's our opportunity to ensure we have the right staff in place to take us to the next step. Trim the fat. Surely you of all people can appreciate that."

Zack leaned back and let his gaze slip from her to the city skyline behind her. He did understand. He hated it, didn't want to be a part of it, but he understood. "How many do we need to let go?"

"We're tackling new hires and those who have questionable performance reviews first. Once they're gone, Nancy figures we'll only need to have managers cut two percent of their teams. And they will have identified those candidates during this week's budget reviews."

Two percent. That would work out to be five or six people from his team. More than he would have liked, but not as bad as it could have been. "Packages?"

"Generous. Enough that no one will mind the early departure."

In the corporate world, there were no guarantees, not anymore. It was hard to let people go, but ensuring they had a generous severance package eased the pain. Hopefully, it would give them enough time to find another job before the money ran out.

Zack pinched the bridge of his nose and sighed. "So the timeline in Friday's email still stands?"

"By end of day tomorrow, you'll need to identify impacted staff. HR will run point, and they'll be packaged out by end of day Thursday."

"I'll have the list to you before then." He pushed himself to his feet, suddenly aware of the weight that pressed down on him. There was nothing worse in the world than having to lay off staff. Knowing he was responsible for the financial breakdown for multiple families was horrible.

Samantha stood as he began to walk away. "Are you okay with this?"

"Not really. But I don't have much of a choice, do I?"

"No, you don't. But look on the bright side. If you can't bear to stay on at Compass yourself, you'll have an awesome separation package when this is all said and done. Enough to open that gym of yours."

His head snapped around so fast, the muscles in his neck screamed. "You know about that?"

She snorted. "Do you honestly think there is anything about my executives that I'm not aware of? I was alerted to your little side project months ago."

For the first time in nearly a decade, he felt like a kid who'd been caught with candy before dinner: ashamed and embarrassed. "It won't change my work ethic. I've always given Compass my top priority."

"Which is the only reason I haven't brought it up before now. Needless to say, if it ever does affect your work here, I'll have another name to add to my list of former employees."

Zack nodded, the message coming across loud and clear. "I'll give you an update by end of day tomorrow."

He couldn't look at her any longer, so he turned and left as quickly as he could.

The elevator was empty, giving him a brief respite from social interaction. He leaned on the back wall, letting his head knock against the paneling as the doors slid shut and the elevator shivered into motion.

God, that was not how he'd hoped that meeting would go. Why had he thought he'd be able to swoop in, demand that Samantha listen to him, and change everything to his liking? Hell, he'd barely gotten a few sentences out before she had him walking over to her side of the argument. She'd had the upper hand all along, because she'd known more than he had. Once he knew all the information, he'd come to the same conclusions as Samantha about what the company needed to do—because it was the logical, efficient course of action.

Zack had always been cursed with seeing the big picture. It was one of the reasons he'd risen as quickly as he had through the ranks. As much as it hurt, excess sometimes had to be trimmed, costs cut, and people let go. The company came before the employees, and larger economic forces were more important than individuals; sometimes executives had to be the face of those larger forces. He'd never taken any joy in those acts, but before now he'd never questioned the validity of them.

For some reason, this time it wasn't sitting right.

The corporate world had always been cutthroat, especially the higher he rose through the ranks. Max had rejected the opportunity to go into big business for himself, claiming that while he might not get rich, at the very least he'd remain in control of his life and stay accountable to the people who relied on him. Zack had always believed he'd been shortsighted, that Max had missed out on too many opportunities to take Frantic to the next level. Maybe Max had been right all along.

Zack hoped Nolan would have a coffee ready for him when he got back to the office. He was going to need all the caffeine he could swallow to get through the next few days with his psyche intact.

The elevator doors slid open on his floor to reveal Nancy, leaning against the wall on one shoulder as she stared down the hall in the direction of his office.

"Nancy?" He stepped out and was surprised when she turned; she'd obviously been crying. "What's wrong? The layoffs?"

She nodded, her gaze dropping to the stack of file folders she clung to. "I hate this."

"It's never pleasant, especially when no one knows it's coming. But we'll get through it. Did you want me to get Nolan to come help?"

It was strange how the thought of losing Nolan hadn't crossed his mind until Nancy looked up at him, wide-eyed. It hadn't even been a blip on his mental radar. But then her lips parted, and the words came out a half second after he guessed what she was going to say. "Nolan's on the list."

Of course he was. He was still a new hire, still under his three-month probation period, putting him on the list of easiest employees to lose.

"No." There had to be a way around this. Samantha had to be willing to cut him some slack, to make an exception. He had not only accepted the need for an assistant now, but had grown so dependent on Nolan he couldn't imagine walking into that office and him not being there. Nolan was important to him, kept him productive and happy. Surely Zack's importance to Compass earned him a bit of leverage in this matter.

"Nancy, don't talk to him yet." He pressed the elevator button, knowing that if he didn't talk to Samantha right now, then this could get out of control quickly. "Do what you have to do next, but not Nolan."

"I fought for him already. She was adamant that all new hires had to go."

"No!" He closed his eyes and sucked in a breath. "No. Go to the next person on the list. Give me time." He ignored the look of pity on her face, turning to step into the elevator the second the doors slid open again. "The next person."

She nodded as the doors closed.

"Fucking ridiculous." He stabbed the floor button and waited to explode through the doors the moment they opened. "Samantha!"

She stood by her assistant's desk, her shoulders rising as he said her name. "I thought you knew what had to be done, Mr. Anderson. I doubt you finished in the five minutes you've been gone."

"Not Nolan."

She turned, but instead of the sympathy he'd hoped to see, there was nothing but annoyance in her expression. "Nancy is taking care of your assistant. I thought it would be better than you having to do the deed yourself."

"There's no reason to let Nolan go. I need him to keep things going in my office."

"Bullshit. You did fine for months without an assistant, you'll survive again." She turned her back to him. "Get on with it, Zack, or I'll be searching for a new CTO."

His hand balled into a fist. "You wouldn't."

"I guess I was too subtle earlier. Let me make it very clear: You have a clause in your contract preventing moonlighting, which your little side project gym qualifies as. If I invoke that clause, you'll end up with nothing, and I'll still let Nolan go." She glanced at him, her gaze cold. "He seems like a capable man. He'll find another job. Compass will get through this, and you'll get stock options or a package. You'll have more than enough money to do what you want. Now, I have to make a call with the board. Good-bye, Zack." She took a file from her assistant, walked into her office, and closed the door.

Zack couldn't move. His legs had gone numb, his chest tight from the anger and frustration that swirled inside him. The poor woman behind the desk kept looking at him, her hand hovering close to her phone.

He cleared his throat. "Don't worry, you won't have to call security."

What the hell was he going to do? He couldn't lose his job, not when it was the only source of support for himself and the gym. But God, Nolan...

He knew how difficult it had been for Nolan to get through the interview, to deal with the stress and anxiety of adjusting to the new position. Zack would have to talk to him, explain the situation, and find a way to make things better.

This time when the elevator opened to reveal his floor, Nancy wasn't there. In Zack's outer office, Nolan was pacing behind his desk, the phone pressed to his ear. No doubt he was running interference for Zack, or booking an appointment, or generally being amazing. Zack took one step, then another toward his office, his gaze locked on the man he'd shared a bed with only a few days earlier.

Had Samantha known they'd slept together? It would certainly explain her resistance to the idea of keeping Nolan on—firing Nolan could be her way of punishing Zack for starting up the gym on the side.

He wouldn't put it past her. He could hear Nolan's voice reverberate through the glass doors the closer he got. The words weren't quite distinguishable, but Zack could hear his tone: pleasant, soothing, and calm.

Nolan looked up and smiled at him as he pushed the office door open. "Thank you. Yes, I'll be sure to add that to his calendar. I'm sorry, I have to go. Yup. You too." He hung up the phone and rounded his desk to approach Zack. "Are you okay? You're pale."

Shit, he was going to have to do this. He couldn't leave it to Nancy. He had to fire Nolan.

"Can you come into my office?" He didn't wait to see if Nolan would follow; he didn't have to. The smell and heat from Nolan's body wrapped around him like a sweater. "Close the door behind you."

It was easy to go on autopilot. He had the routine down pat; he'd let so many people go over the years. Though never someone he'd slept with.

Never someone he had feelings for.

Nolan moved to the guest chair, but didn't sit down. "Zack, are you okay? What did Ms. Rollins say?"

Zack stepped behind his desk, but rather than sit, he turned to look out the window. "She knows about the gym."

"Ah, that's bad, right?"

"I have a noncompete clause in my contract with a moonlighting subsection. I can be terminated for any side businesses I start. I was told initially that was to prevent me from starting a consulting business while I was still employed, but Samantha informed me it applies to the gym as well."

"Shit. Is she going to fire you?" There was fear and a bit of anger in his voice. Sweet, but totally misplaced.

"No. She expects me to do my job. As long as I toe the company line, she'll overlook the gym."

"Well, that's good." Nolan came up behind him and placed a hand on his shoulder. "What's wrong?"

The scent of Nolan's cologne had faded from the morning, and now blended in with the milder smells of fabric softener, antiperspirant, and the raw scent of Nolan. Zack turned, almost pressing his nose to Nolan's neck to breathe it in. Instead, he looked into those beautiful hazel eyes and forced himself to take a step back.

Nolan frowned. "Zack?"

He couldn't do this. He couldn't say the words that he knew damn well he had to. But he'd struggled too hard to get to this point, and he needed the money his position at Compass offered so he could reopen the gym. That was truly his heart's work. Nolan would understand.

"You're scaring me." Nolan reached out for him, but Zack took another step back.

"I'm sorry."

"For what? If you don't tell me what's going on, then I can't help—"

Autopilot. "Nolan, I want you to know that you've done excellent work in your time here at Compass."

"Thank you." Nolan shoved his hands into his pockets. "But?"

"But I'm sorry to inform you that due to some recent changes, management has no choice but to terminate all new hires who are still under their three-month evaluation period. It isn't a reflection on your performance, and I will be happy to provide you with a reference."

He never once looked away from Nolan, so it was easy to see the joy in his eyes snuff out. The pulse point in Nolan's neck began to throb hard, and the color drained from his face. "Wait . . . you're serious."

"You weren't singled out, if you're worried about that. New hires were the easiest to target and had the least financial impact for Compass. Nancy has the necessary paperwork, but I thought it best that you hear it from me."

Nolan swallowed hard and reached out for the desk to steady himself. "Did you try to keep me?"

"Samantha made it very clear. I either go along with the reorganization, or I'm shown the door as well. I'd lose my income and the chance to open the gym."

"So it was me or you." Nolan's breathing grew labored, and his body started to shake. "Well, it's good to know where I stand."

"It wasn't like that. If I'd kicked up a fuss, she would have fired me *too*, but either way you'd still be rolled up in the layoffs. My hands are tied here."

Nolan took a shaky step away. "But you didn't even try to fight for me."

"Nolan—"

"Don't. Just . . ." He stumbled briefly before righting himself. "I'll leave."

"Let me take you home."

"No."

"You're having a panic attack."

"It's anxiety, not panic. I just lost my job, why wouldn't I be anxious? I'm fine. I'll call . . . I'm fine."

Nolan had been doing so well that Zack had never considered the news would trigger an attack. But of course it had; even somebody without anxiety would be devastated to get fired with no warning. Especially somebody as conscientious and hardworking as Nolan.

Zack's heart ached to see this kind soul tearing himself apart. "Please, let me at least call you a cab. I need to know that you get home okay."

Nolan let out a strangled laugh. "Well, I'd hate to burden your conscience. Call me a cab, then. I'll leave right away."

Without another look at him, Nolan gathered his things and left the office for good.

CHAPTER NINETEEN

Whether it was by luck or Zack making good on his offer, there was a cab waiting at the curb by the time Nolan stumbled out of the building. He'd thrown his security badge on the desk as he passed, but for the life of him, he didn't notice who'd been sitting there. His world was spinning, and nothing made sense.

Zack had fired him.

He gave his address to the driver, closed his eyes, and tried to run through his breathing techniques. They weren't helping. How could they, when his entire world had fallen apart around him in a matter of seconds? He'd lost his job and most likely the man he was starting to have feelings for. Not that Zack had said anything about their personal relationship, but Nolan couldn't imagine that they'd be able to continue forward after this.

What the hell did they have in common outside of work?

He didn't have a clue. They'd spent hours together, and Nolan had managed numerous aspects of Zack's life, but he knew next to nothing about him.

That wasn't true.

He knew that Zack used his anger like a shield to protect himself, and wielded it like a sword to slay the demons sent to hurt him. Nolan could picture a younger Zack, scared and angry, working out at the gym, learning to control that prominent feature of his personality rather than let it control him. Nolan had gone through much the same process over the past few years, doing his best to learn how to handle his anxiety. Neither of them seemed to have mastered their emotions.

Nolan needed to get home and take an extra clonazepam and hope that would do the trick. Where techniques and practice and willpower failed him, modern medicine usually succeeded.

When the taxi pulled up, he tapped his Visa on the machine and stumbled out onto the sidewalk. He wanted nothing more than to climb into bed and stay there until the horrors of his current reality faded. Grabbing the mail from his slot didn't help matters, seeing as most of the envelopes contained bills that he no longer knew how he'd pay.

Of all the things that could have happened today, losing his job wasn't something he'd seen coming. How could he have? Apparently even Zack hadn't known. Or at least Nolan assumed that, but really, he had no idea what to assume or believe about Zack anymore. Maybe Zack had been sitting on that news for days.

The quiet of his apartment, while normally inviting, pressed down on him. The place was one more financial concern he suddenly faced. He'd only officially taken over the lease from Tina the previous week, and there wasn't an easy way for him to break it now.

Tina. He couldn't believe that his first reaction after Zack told him that he was being let go was to call his big sister. Here he'd been thinking things were finally getting better, that for the first time since the accident he was ready to handle everything on his own. What a joke. *He* was a joke.

The bed was too far away, so he fell onto the couch, setting the stack of bills on the cushion beside him. His cell phone was still deep in his pocket, digging into his bad leg. He pulled it free and pressed the Home button. "Call Tina."

She answered after only a few rings. "Hello, brother." Her voice brought a smile to his face. "You have good timing. I just finished getting dressed."

He was never going to get used to her being in a different time zone. "What time is it there?"

"Eight. I have a half hour before I head out to work."

"That's good."

"It is. So what's wrong?"

"Why would you think something's wrong? Can't I just call my big sister? Maybe I missed you."

"Dude, it's lunch there. You're usually run off your feet in the middle of the day. You don't sound like you do when you're having an anxiety attack, so I have to assume there's something else going on. So tell me."

His chest hurt, and he realized he hadn't taken his pill. He bumped into the coffee table on his way to the bathroom.

"Nolan?"

"Just having a bad day."

"Are you okay? You sound off."

The rush of water made it hard for him to hear what she said next. He fumbled for his pill, knowing that it wouldn't work instantly, but it would help set him straight for the rest of the day.

"Nolan, hon, you're scaring me. Do I need to call Mom to come check on you?"

"Shit, don't do that."

"Well then tell me what's going on. You called me for a reason."

God, he'd missed her, the way she was able to get right to the heart of him and take control. "Zack fired me."

"*What?*"

"Well, not fired. There were some layoffs at work. They got rid of all new hires to save money."

"That asshole! And here I thought he was a good one."

"It wasn't his fault. I don't think he had much say in things."

"He's the frigging CTO, I'm sure he has more pull than that."

Nolan leaned one hand on the bathroom counter and closed his eyes. Replaying the scene in his mind, he felt guilty for his earlier moment of suspicion; it was obvious Zack had been just as miserable as he was. Why had he been so willing to doubt Zack's motives? "Seriously, Tina. You didn't see his face. He didn't want to be doing it, and I've seen him fire people. I don't know exactly what happened."

"Where are you right now?"

"In the bathroom. I just took a pill."

"Okay, good. You need to lie down and rest."

He wanted to cry, but somehow he managed to hold back the tears. "I need to find another job so I don't miss next month's rent."

"You'll find one. But that doesn't matter right now. Go rest. Sleep this off until the anxiety passes. Then you can figure out your next move."

He knew she was right, and that he was in no condition to be able to fix this problem right now. Too bad his brain wouldn't stop the merry-go-round of worry and blame, spinning his fear and panic into a vortex.

"Nolan?"

"I'll go lie down."

"I'm going to let Mom know what's going on."

"No. Please don't."

"I need to—"

"No, you don't. I'm an adult, and I need to learn how to manage these moments on my own. I can't keep running to you or Mom and Dad every time I have an issue."

Tina's frustration came through loud and clear in her sigh. "You don't have to go through this alone."

It was strange, but since Tina had moved and he'd thrown himself into his job, he'd felt as though he was finally taking control of his life. Now her concern seemed less well-intentioned than insulting. Of course he could handle things himself, just as he had before the accident. Of course he was a fully functional person again, able to manage his own affairs. His attitude had changed so much in such a short time.

It hadn't hurt that the more time he'd spent with Zack, the more his world had opened up.

Had it only been a few days since they'd made love at Zack's place? Those memories, still fresh, tangible, were something he could cling to. Better that than recalling the look of frustration and anger Zack had worn while he delivered the news. While their relationship as boss and assistant might be over, that didn't mean *they* had to be done.

He cleared his throat and looked at himself in the mirror. "I'm not alone."

"Now I'm going to worry about you all day."

"Don't. I'm home and I'm fine. You're right: I'm going to have a nap and then tackle this when my mind is clear. I just needed to hear your voice. I miss you."

"I miss you too." She paused, and he could hear her shuffling something on the other end. "In fact, I'm glad you called. Mind you, not about the reason, but I'm happy to talk to you. I've been finding things hard. Out here. Alone."

Ever since they were kids, Tina had always come across as the untouchable one; she had an iron will and let nothing get in the way of what she wanted. Hearing her admit that her move was harder than she'd expected broke his heart.

"I know you're heading to work soon, but how about later we do a Skype call? I think we could both use some face time."

"Oh that would be awesome. And since you're not working, you could always come out here. I mean, there are jobs in Vancouver, and my place here is actually a two-bedroom. It would be like old times."

The thought of leaving Toronto, of leaving Zack, hurt. Then again, they had made no commitments. They weren't a couple and hadn't even established whether they'd be seeing each other again after the interlude at Zack's house. They'd had great sex, then Zack had checked his email for five minutes, and the next thing Nolan knew his world was turned upside down. While the thought of packing up and heading halfway across the country was slightly terrifying, at least with Tina he knew exactly what to expect.

"I'll think about it, and we can talk more tonight." His anxiety relaxed, though whether from his conversation with Tina or the early effects of the pills kicking in, he couldn't be certain. "I love you."

"Love you too. I'll ping you later."

Hanging up, he took the opportunity to splash water on his face before making his way to the bedroom. He hadn't finished setting things up yet; half of his belongings were still in boxes down in the storage space. The barren walls and half-made bed gave the impression of a person in transition. The room held no personal effects, but was waiting to take on some life. It was strangely similar to Zack's home, though his place was far neater than Nolan managed. No doubt, Zack had cleaners to help keep things tidy.

Zack.

He fell onto the bed and closed his eyes. It shouldn't be weighing on him this much, not knowing where he stood with his sort-of lover. Shit, he should be more worried about the fact that he was going to have to look for a job again. The experience he'd gained from his short tenure at Compass would help, but the prospect of sending out résumés, going to interviews, making new friends . . . and doing it all alone . . .

That should be his concern. But the more he thought about what was really upsetting him, the more he knew it had nothing to do with needing to find a new job and everything to do with the thought of Zack no longer being a part of his daily life. He had loved coming into the office in the morning and watching the tension in Zack bleed away. Knowing Zack, Nolan doubted he was even aware of the subtle change. Like the way his lips would twitch up into a small smirk whenever Nolan brought him a coffee. Or the way he'd linger behind Nolan's chair, standing closer than he should while they spoke.

The smell of Zack's aftershave, his shampoo, hell, even the scent of his detergent were burned into Nolan's brain. And the memories of Zack's body, the way he touched Nolan's scars, kissed them with reverence as he aroused the rest of him—no one had ever treated him with such passion and love.

Nolan sat bolt upright, his heart pounding hard.

Love. No, there was no way Zack was in love with him. Lust, no doubt about it. But *love*?

With shaking hands, he pushed his hair from his face. The real question wasn't what Zack felt, but rather what Nolan felt for him.

Was it more than simple friends with benefits?

Yeah. It really was.

Shit.

He had to find Zack and talk to him about everything that had happened. He'd left so quickly, in such a panic, he hadn't even considered that they had more to discuss than what was happening at Compass.

Nolan had lost his job, and that was undeniably awful. But Zack's world had been shaken up too, and Nolan hadn't spared a thought for him until hours later. What exactly had Samantha Rollins threatened him with? Would he have to give up the gym entirely? Was there a chance he might actually leave Compass? Nolan should have asked him questions instead of reacting, but panic had taken over his brain.

No . . . He knew the anxiety was real, but he couldn't place all the blame on his condition any more than he could ignore it and make it go away. He had to live with it, and that included taking responsibility for how he treated the people he cared about. Possibly loved.

Now he was stuck, though. After the way they'd left things unfinished, should he call Zack or wait for him to call? Neither felt ideal. Maybe he needed more time.

If nothing else, he did have something to keep him busy while he looked for a new job. He might have been fired from Compass, but he could still follow through on his commitments to Ringside. And making progress there might be the perfect way to show Zack they had a future outside the company. If not, it was still the right thing to do.

Unfortunately, when he tried Zack's office, he got his own outdated Compass voice mail. He slapped his forehead and dialed again, using Zack's direct extension. More voice mail. After a moment of hesitation, he tried Zack's cell phone. It went straight to voice mail without even ringing.

Nolan hung up with a big question mark floating in his mind. Was Zack out somewhere away from his office, too busy or upset to even pick up his phone, or was he ignoring the calls deliberately? Would he want to hear anything Nolan had to say about Ringside, now that Nolan was no longer his assistant at Compass?

Picking up his cell phone again, Nolan called the one person he knew would have the answers.

"Hi there. May I speak with Max, please?"

Nolan hadn't been back to Frantic since his disastrous night out with Tina. There'd been no point in courting another incident when he was clearly not ready. But seeing the bar in the daytime put it in a strange light for him; it was less torture house and more warehouse.

After a brief phone call, Max had suggested Nolan come down to the bar so they could talk face-to-face. So there he stood, staring up at the unlit sign and trying to screw up enough courage to go in.

"Coming through."

Nolan jumped out of the way of two men with their arms full of what appeared to be sound equipment. "Let me get the door for you."

Well, no point in opening the door and then not going in. Nolan followed the men in, ignoring the sudden pounding of his heart.

There were several people milling around, clearly getting ready to open. Three people stood behind the bar: two men and a woman who was currently laughing at the taller of the two.

The taller man turned his head and grinned the moment he saw him. "Nolan! Come over."

He knew he'd met Max, but this man didn't look even a bit familiar. All Nolan remembered was his voice, deep and warm. "Is this a bad time? I can come back later."

Max came out from behind the bar, revealing even more of his impressive frame. Zack was fairly tall, but Max was huge. "Later it'll be a zoo and I won't have five minutes to myself. Let's go back to the office."

Nolan trailed behind him, throwing a small smile to the two remaining bartenders as he passed. As he went, he tried to take stock of everything he saw, but there was nothing outstanding about the building when it wasn't lit up with the pulse of music flowing through it. Strange how someplace so innocuous could have caused him so much hurt.

Sort of like a tree in a ditch.

"Have a seat. Can I get you anything? Beer, water?"

"I'm good, thanks. How's your mom?"

"Much better. Nothing like being waited on hand and foot by her only son to brighten her spirits." Max fell into his chair behind the desk, laced his hands behind his head, and leaned back. "So, Zack fired you."

"He did."

"Did he have a choice?"

"No. I accused him of not fighting for me, but I know that wasn't true." He'd even reached out to Nancy, and she'd been nothing but regretful about the circumstances. She'd had no clue where Zack was that day, however.

"He can be a prick, but he's a loyal prick. You won him over pretty fucking fast. If there was anything he could have done to save your job, rest assured he would have done it."

Nolan's gaze slipped to his hands. "I know. I was hurting and lashed out at him."

"I wouldn't worry about it. Zack can stand to be on the receiving end of someone else's anger for once. It might wake him up. So . . . you're unemployed."

"Yup." Nolan took a deep breath and straightened. "But I'm not without a job."

"Oh?" Max let his hands fall to the desk. "You mean Ringside."

"I do. Zack asked me to help, and I plan to keep my end of the bargain."

"So what was this plan of yours that you wanted to discuss with me?"

It was possible Max would balk at his big idea, but Nolan was fairly confident he'd be on board with one of the smaller pitches. "Ringside needs money. I want to use Frantic to run a fund-raiser."

Max's eyes widened for a moment before he broke out in a grin. "I knew you were a smart one. Why the hell didn't we think of that? It's so simple."

"You're focused on Frantic, and Zack is preoccupied with his job. Sometimes it's easier to see these things from the outside. It's only a start and won't be enough, but it will raise awareness. Which is another thing I was thinking about."

As soon as he started, Nolan couldn't stop the flood of ideas from coming. A marketing campaign, outreach to community groups, government grants for small businesses. There were so many options out there for them to take a run at, he had no doubt some would be successful.

"The problem the two of you have is time," he finally said, taking a deep breath before bringing out his main suggestion. "You need a project manager."

Max chuckled. "I told Zack you'd have him so organized he wouldn't know what hit him. That seems like a natural transition. So what do you need from me, besides the club?"

It shouldn't be a nerve-racking thing, but the words stuck in his mouth. With a groan, Nolan rubbed at his thigh. "I need Zack to agree to this."

"So ask him."

"I . . . don't know how. I know it's stupid, but we've only known each other a month, and it wasn't as though we were friends. He was my boss, and Ringside is his dream." And Max might or might not know any more than that about their relationship; Nolan didn't want to reveal anything Zack had been trying to keep from Max. Leaning forward, he shook his head. "I guess I just need to know that I'm not overstepping here. I inserted myself into this, first offered to help, because of work. I'd like to stay on at Ringside even if it's as a volunteer, but I think I could be a great project manager, and I had the idea before I knew I'd be losing my job at Compass. You know him better than me. I just wanted to be certain."

Max stood and came around to the other side of the desk to perch on the edge. "You're right, I do know him better. The last time I saw him he was sitting in the same chair you are. He was drinking because of you. He'd done something stupid, which isn't abnormal. But he was sulking, which is far from typical Zack behavior."

In the little over a month he'd known Zack, sulking wasn't a thing Nolan had seen even once. "That's weird."

"I thought so too, until I realized he was upset because he thought he'd hurt you. Zack isn't intuitive when it comes to people's emotions. He can brush them aside, which is great when you're a CTO needing to make major corporate decisions. It's not so wonderful when you like someone."

Nolan's stomach flipped. "You say that like we're kids."

"Zack is in some ways. He never seriously dated anyone when we were younger. Then he didn't have time. You're the first man I've ever seen him interested in. So if you're asking me if I think Zack will have a problem with you wanting to continue to be a part of his life and help him with Ringside, then no, I don't think there will be an issue."

"Oh. Okay." Nolan got to his feet and did his best to ignore the nervous tremor that rolled through him. "I guess that means I need to talk to him."

"I guess so. You're a good man, and you're good for him. He's not the easiest person to get along with, but once you get through his shell, he's got a huge heart."

"I know. You wouldn't happen to know where he is, would you? I've tried him at the office and on his cell, but either he isn't in, he can't hear his phone, or he doesn't want to talk to me."

Max chuckled. "I would lay odds it is anything but that last one. Think about it. Does he really strike you as the silent-treatment type?"

"Ah." Nolan flushed with relief. "No, I guess not."

"I don't know where he is, though. Sorry. If he gets in touch, I'll tell him you're looking for him."

"Okay. Thanks, Max." He shook Max's hand. "I'll keep you posted."

Max smiled. "I'm sure Zack will beat you to that, if all goes the way I suspect it will. Good luck."

Nolan walked out of Frantic, his brain spinning and his heart pounding. Zack cared for him, he knew it. All he had to do was hope that Zack would be willing to let Nolan in, accept him as more than an assistant. Nolan wanted his heart.

CHAPTER TWENTY

Zack stood in front of the old, musty heavy bag that one of the teens must have discovered while they'd been cleaning the gym. It wasn't any good at all, but based on the amount of dust that had gathered beneath where it now hung, at least a few of the teens had taken some punches.

He'd tried to stay late at the office and get some work done, but eventually he'd given up. He'd needed a place he could yell and scream without fear of scaring the shit out of anyone. Getting to vent his anger on the heavy bag was an unexpected bonus.

When he'd arrived, none of the high school kids were around, but the contractor had been there. Zack had been forced to keep things bottled up long enough to make small talk and quickly discuss the work plan. Nothing major was starting for at least a month, and even then it would only be a fraction of the work that needed to happen before Ringside could open.

The moment the contractor left, Zack counted to ten before letting out a tremendous yell. He was sick and tired of things not going his way. He'd worked long and hard, but he couldn't continue to bear up under this constant barrage of hits. Even the best fighter couldn't always get up from the mat after a beating.

He missed Nolan. Hated what he'd done to him.

Stripping off his shirt, Zack hung it on a nail jutting from the wall. An envelope fell from the pocket, and Zack snatched it from the floor and rubbed his thumb over the seal before folding it and replacing it. He'd impulsively grabbed Miranda's letter from his desk drawer before he left the office, after forwarding the to-be-terminated list to Samantha. It was time to suck it up and read the thing. After seeing it and choosing to ignore it countless times, he'd decided he owed his former employee that much.

Just . . . not now.

Next went his watch, which he carefully tucked into the pocket of his shirt. He turned and tried to relax his jaw. Shit, his teeth were clenched so hard his head was pounding.

Fuck it.

Without any sort of finesse, he got into his stance, pulled his bare fist back, and slammed it into the bag. Pain immediately exploded across his unprotected skin where it connected with the damaged canvas. He didn't care. Another jab, this time followed by a cross. Then another. And another, until he couldn't feel anything but the pain in his hands.

He kept going.

Dust filled the air, making it difficult to breathe properly. And he kept going. It was only when his knuckles began to mark the bag with blood that he finally let his hands fall to his sides and stumbled backward. Sweat and dirt covered his torso in muddy streaks, and blood welled up bright and thick on his hands. He didn't care. He knew he deserved every bit of pain for all the suffering he'd caused others over the years.

His parents, Miranda, Nolan, the team members whose fate he'd decided today; they all deserved better than what he could give.

He caught sight of the letter poking out of his shirt pocket, and marched over. If Miranda had wanted him to know her thoughts before she died, then he would damn well give her that honor. He tore into the envelope, yanked the contents free, and started reading. When he was halfway through, his legs gave out on him and he sat down on the floor. He pressed the heel of his hand to his eye and started the letter again.

Dear Mr. Anderson,

By now, I'm sure you've learned that I've made the decision to take my own life. Most people say this is the coward's way out, and maybe they're right. But I've never been a particularly brave person, so it seems fitting.

I've been sick for a long time. Not just physically, though I have my problems, but mentally. My sister is a wonderful person, but the weight of her personality was too much for me. I always needed to keep up, to find a way to be better. I started stealing when I was younger. As long as I didn't get caught, it gave me a rush, made me feel special, different from her. It was my way of sticking it to people I didn't like. I hated myself for needing to do that. I still do. I had to steal, but at least I could usually control who I stole from and tell myself they deserved it.

When I first came to work for you, I hated you immediately. You were an asshole who didn't care about anyone. Day one I took your stapler and stashed it in my car. You didn't even notice. Then I took the laptop. When you caught me and you believed my story, I thought you were an idiot. But when you fired me, I wasn't surprised.

What did catch me off guard was what you said to me before security escorted me out of the building. I wonder if you even remember.

Zack did remember. She'd looked so sad that day, as though she'd lost more than her job. He'd put a hand on her shoulder and simply said, *"You're a good person. Don't give up on yourself."*

It wasn't anything earth-shattering as far as comfort went, and in the end it hadn't been nearly enough. But something had resonated enough with her that one of her final acts was to write him this letter.

It doesn't really matter if you do or not. I remember. Those words stuck with me for a long time. When the police didn't show up for me and I knew you hadn't turned me in, I felt even more ashamed. I tried to get better, do better after that. Worked harder in therapy, got back on meds. A part of me wanted to make you proud.

I'm writing this letter to say that I'm sorry I gave up, but the world was just too hard. You're a good person too, Mr. Anderson. Thank you for your kindness.

Miranda.

Zack read the letter over a few more times until the words were burned into his brain. The poor woman had tried to turn her life around alone. He couldn't imagine dealing with that sort of pain without someone to talk to, to help him work through the anger and frustration. Russel had seen the pain lingering below his skin as a teen and done everything he could to get Zack on the right path.

Zack could only imagine Nolan had gone through much the same thing after his accident, relying on help from scores of doctors, therapists, and family members to piece his body and mind back together.

Nolan.

Zack closed his eyes and hoped Nolan was okay. When he'd left the office, Nolan was beyond rattled. With his sister in Vancouver, he would be alone if he had one of his attacks. Zack wanted nothing more than to go to his apartment and check in on him. Be the person he relied on for help. But given the way Nolan had looked at him, the things he'd said, that would undoubtedly be a bad idea. So he'd come here instead.

The throbbing in his hands was getting worse, forcing Zack to finally move. He'd picked up a large first aid kit for the gym office a few weeks earlier, and it was still sitting in the corner of the main room next to a stack of protective goggles and some other safety gear the kids had been using while they worked. Carefully popping the giant plastic box open, he saw that all the bandages and cleaning supplies were still wrapped in plastic.

"Shit." His fingers were too painful to move much. Picking up the bandage pack, he tried to tear into it with his teeth as he gingerly held it with both palms.

"What the hell did you do?"

The package fell to the floor as Zack spun around, then froze. Nolan was coming toward him, dressed in jeans and a T-shirt that hung loose on his too slight frame. Zack couldn't move, even when Nolan bent down and picked up the package, ripped it open, and took out a spool of sterile gauze.

"God, you've destroyed your hands. Is there any peroxide?" Nolan didn't wait for him to answer, instead dug through the first aid kit to retrieve the supplies he needed. "If we don't get the dirt out of it, you're going to get an infection."

Zack let Nolan take his hands out so they hovered between them. "Why are you here?"

Nolan flashed him a scowl. "Apparently to clean you up. Don't move."

After cracking open the seal on the peroxide, Nolan poured a generous amount across his knuckles.

White bubbles fizzed up, obscuring his skin and the cuts. Zack sucked in a breath at the sting. "Shit, that hurts."

"It would hurt more if it was alcohol. What were you doing? If there's something that can hurt the kids, I need to let their teacher and the contractor know before they come back next week."

Ignoring the pain, he took Nolan's hands in his. "Stop."

Nolan's eyes went wide. "You're bleeding."

"I'm fine."

Nolan cleared his throat as his gaze slipped away to a point behind Zack. "You were boxing?"

"I was. That happens here."

When Nolan's gaze returned to Zack, it was actually funny. His eyes widened, and his mouth fell open. "You're not wearing a shirt."

"Took it off to hit things."

"You're sweaty. And dirty."

"I'll shower later."

"That's probably mold, if it came from that old bag. You should get cleaned up so you don't breathe too much of that—"

"Nolan."

"Yes?"

"Why are you here?" Even as he asked, he realized he almost didn't care why. He was just glad to see him, touch him, hear his voice and know Nolan was all right.

Nolan stepped back, rubbing one hand along the back of his neck. "I wanted to talk to you. When I called the office and your cell and you didn't pick up, I thought I'd try here. Well, first stop was Frantic. The club, not my state of mind." A blush crept up Nolan's cheeks. "Do you mind putting something on? I can't talk to you when you're looking all . . ." He waved his hand around Zack's chest, as though that said it all.

The anger and frustration that had grabbed Zack in a python's grip began to release. "Sure. Give me a second."

His dress shirt was dark, so at the very least it wouldn't be ruined by the sweat, blood, and dirt. He ignored Nolan and took his time doing up the buttons of his shirt, needing a few moments to wrap his head around what was going on. Because it really did matter why Nolan was here.

Okay, Nolan had come looking for him. He was willing to go to multiple locations so they could have a face-to-face conversation. That had to be a good thing, right? Maybe he wasn't as angry at Zack as Zack had first assumed.

"Jesus."

He turned around to see Nolan holding Miranda's letter. "Put that down."

"I'm sorry, I didn't mean to—"

"Now." He let out a huff. "Please."

Nolan folded the note in half and held it out for him to take. "Did you do that to yourself before or after you read her note?"

"Before."

Nolan frowned. "Why?"

Seeing him standing there, Zack was beginning to wonder the same thing. "I was angry at myself for what I had to do to you."

"You didn't have a choice. I know that now." He gave a little shrug. "I have some savings that will cover my rent and expenses for a month or two. I should be able to find another job by then."

Another job, where Zack wouldn't see him every day. But that was how things had to be. "I'll do whatever I can to help you."

"That was actually one of the things I wanted to talk to you about." Nolan glanced at Zack's hands again. "And I'll be happy to tell you if you let me wrap those up."

Zack could continue to be stubborn, but it was hard to maintain the edge when Nolan was standing there looking cute but stern. "Sure."

They moved to the rickety old bench by the wall, where Zack sat and held his hands out.

Nolan squatted in front of him, lifting the edge of the gauze from the spool. "I spoke to Max."

"What? When?"

"About an hour ago. I wanted to run something by him before I brought it to you. Someone who knew you and the situation."

Nolan's hands were gentle as he wrapped gauze around the wounds. Zack shifted so their faces were closer. "What's that?"

"I want to be the project manager for Ringside." Nolan cast him a quick glance, but continued. "What I'm proposing is this: I'll come on and look after the construction, organize the fund-raising, and oversee grant applications. If I'm able to make progress, and if we get some money, then I'd like to ask for a small salary. Just enough to make sure I don't get thrown out of my place or starve. You can't do this and your job at Compass. It's too much for one person. Max means well, but he has a business of his own to handle. Though I do have plans to use Frantic as a base to launch some fund-raising, but we can talk about that later. There, one done."

Zack let his bandaged hand fall to his lap and held the other one up. "I'm surprised you want anything to do with me at all."

"What do you mean? Ringside has so much potential, both as a gym and as a chance to give teens a safe place to figure things out. You know how much it helped you. I wish I'd known about it when I was younger. A chance to be a part of rebuilding that would be a privilege." Nolan finished fixing Zack's hand before he slid his own onto Zack's thighs. "And it will give me a chance to spend time with you."

"My previous statement still stands."

"Why? Because you were forced to fire me? Don't be an ass." Nolan tightened his grip on him. "You were the first person in over two years to treat me like a person. You didn't let my disability define or limit what you believed I could accomplish. You pushed me, yelled at me, treated me exactly the way you'd treat anyone else. Did I have a few setbacks? Sure. But even so, I feel more like my old self. I even looked in the mirror this morning and didn't hate what I saw staring back at me."

God, how could anyone hate anything about you? Zack cupped Nolan's face with his bandaged hands. "I'm glad I fired you."

"You are?" Nolan's voice shook. "Why?"

"So I can do this and not worry."

The kiss was unlike anything he'd shared with anyone else. Love welled up, all-encompassing and bright. The scrape of stubble against his face sent chills through him, making every cell in his body burst with awareness. The swipe of his tongue against Nolan's had them both groaning, clawing at each other to get closer. He pulled at Nolan's shoulders until Nolan climbed into his lap.

Now that they were at the same level, it was far easier for him to bury his fingers in Nolan's hair. His fingertips brushed against the scar hidden beneath the surface. Nolan stiffened for a moment, so Zack deepened the kiss as he deliberately traced the ragged trail.

"You're the bravest man I've ever met." Zack nipped Nolan's chin. "And I still don't even know what happened to you."

Nolan's lids were heavy and his lips swollen from their kiss. "Do you want to know? It's not pleasant."

"Tell me."

So, sitting on his lap in a defunct boxing gym, Nolan Carmichael told him every detail of the horrific accident that had forever changed his life. And Zack Anderson, frustrated, angry, and sometimes dragon-like, fell in love.

≡ EPILOGUE ≡

The gym was a zoo. Or it could have passed as one, given how many people were currently careening around Nolan. Sawdust-coated teens carried lumber and tools around the perimeter of the room, hammered away at the framework of the center ring platform, and scrubbed away the final decades of grime and old paint from the walls. Seated on a pair of overturned plastic buckets, a pair of future interior design consultants pored over a booklet of paint swatches, happily debating about the best shade of something called "greige."

They'd made tremendous progress on Ringside in the four months since he'd come on as project manager. Not that he was completely responsible for the success; Zack had worked hard as well.

He'd be working even more soon; he'd officially resigned as CTO of Compass the previous week.

"Nolan?" François, the contractor, sauntered over. "Did you have a chance to review the list of trades I want to use?"

He'd learned so much about contracting it was terrifying. Not that he understood it all—that was why he had François. "You've worked with them all before?"

"They're my normal crew. I trust them."

"And I trust you. When will they start?"

He fought the urge to check the time again, though it was hard to avoid given the giant-ass clock they'd installed on the back wall. The second hand ticked away, taunting him by seeming to slow down, stretching out the interval before he knew Zack was due to arrive.

Considering how much Zack had needed Nolan's help when they'd first met, it was strange how quickly Nolan had come to rely on Zack as well. Not regarding things like healthy workplace communication or empowering team dynamics—their boss-assistant days were well behind them—but rather in little ways.

He loved how Zack made him coffee and brought it to bed first thing in the morning. He adored the way Zack refused to treat him differently than anyone else, but was there with a supporting hand the instant Nolan indicated a need for help. And he could no longer do without those moments in bed when brash, impulsive Zack placed kisses across every one of his scars . . . and slowly, patiently, mended his heart.

François looked around at the calamitous bustle. "It's too quiet here. Where's your partner?"

Yes, Zack might no longer be Nolan's boss, but that didn't mean he wasn't up to bossing everyone else around. "He'll be back soon. I sent him on errands this morning. Figured you'd appreciate having him out of your hair for a while."

"Sure you can't convince him to go back to work?" The Frenchman chuckled. "Those kids will want lunch soon. I think they have some sort of thank-you planned."

"Oh right. I forgot this was their last week."

"They've had a great time and learned a lot. If it's okay with you, I'll give them a bit longer today."

"Yes. Actually, take them over to the Pear Tree for lunch, and charge it to our tab. I'll call ahead to let them know you're coming. A little thank-you from us."

It was then that Zack returned. Strange how Nolan could tell without seeing. The air in the room changed, became charged with the excess energy that floated from him. "Why don't you head over now?"

François winked. "Will do. Children, pack up. Mr. Carmichael was so annoyed with you that he's sending you to lunch early. His treat."

Zack stood to the side as the teens left, banging against one another and laughing as they went. Before long it was just the two of them.

"Our treat?" Zack lifted an eyebrow. "That's going to be expensive."

"I'll take it out of my grocery bill." He leaned in and gave Zack a quick kiss. "Did you find everything okay?"

"I did."

"I only wanted a few paint samples. I figured you would be back long before now." It was weird, but Zack seemed nervous. That couldn't be right. "Are you okay?"

"Yup." Zack let out a little sigh and reached into his pocket. "I was hoping you might be interested in having this."

The object glinted from the overhead lights. Nolan looked at it, then looked again to be certain it was what he thought it was. "A key?"

"To my condo. I figured you spend three or four nights a week there now, you might like to be able to come and go whenever you'd like."

"To your place?"

"You could even move a few of your things in. More than a spare toothbrush and toiletries. Clothes. Books. Some of your physio equipment. I could set up the spare room as a place for you to work out." Zack licked his lips. "If you'd like."

"Are you . . ." Nolan took the key and held it in his hand. "Are you asking me to move in with you?"

"Yes." Zack cupped the back of his head and kissed him softly. "I haven't been this happy before in my life. Even Max said so. I can't wait to see you every day. I need you. You've become the strongest drug in the world. I'm an addict, and I never want to be cured. Move in with me. Please."

Tears welled up in Nolan's eyes, and for a moment he didn't know if he could speak. "What about my place? I signed a yearlong lease. God, I need to call Tina. She'll freak."

"We'll find someone to sublet, or see if you can find someone to take the lease over. Worst case, we'll keep it until you can get out of it. I don't care, we'll make it work." Zack slid his hand to the base of Nolan's spine. "So is that a yes?"

Joy exploded through him. "Of course it's a yes."

"You should know I'm a bit tough to live with." Zack smiled. "I have a bad habit of playing pranks."

Nolan followed his gaze, then jumped back with a scream. "Asshole!"

There in the middle of the ring was the largest stuffed spider he'd ever seen. Zack doubled over, laughing. "Your face!"

Hiding a smirk, Nolan pocketed the key. There were many skills he'd picked up being a project manager, and planning ahead for revenge was one of them. "You're going to regret that."

Zack straightened, his face red from laughter. "I can't wait."

Six months ago, when he'd met Zack for the first time, Nolan could never have imagined him laughing, looking so happy. Somehow they'd clicked—the broken man and the angry one—and become the best team.

No doubt, getting used to stuffed spiders was going to be part of the adventure of living with Zack. "What's this one's name?"

"Biff?"

"That's a stupid name for a spider."

"Don't upset him. Ralph will eat your face off."

"I love you." He kissed Zack on the cheek. "But if you buy me any more of those damned things, there will be serious payback."

Zack blinked at him. "I love you too. What sort of payback?"

He'd been holding this ace in the hole for weeks now. He wandered over to the first aid kit and dug around before pulling out a rubber rat and tossing it at Zack.

Zack jumped back at least three feet. "Shit!"

And Nolan laughed. Life was going to be awesome.

Dear Reader,

Thank you for reading Christine d'Abo's *Working It*!

We know your time is precious and you have many, many entertainment options, so it means a lot that you've chosen to spend your time reading. We really hope you enjoyed it.

We'd be honored if you'd consider posting a review—good or bad—on sites like **Amazon, Barnes & Noble, Kobo, Goodreads, Twitter, Facebook, Tumblr,** and your blog or website. We'd also be honored if you told your friends and family about this book. Word of mouth is a book's lifeblood!

For more information on upcoming releases, author interviews, blog tours, contests, giveaways, and more, please sign up for our weekly, spam-free newsletter and visit us around the web:

Newsletter: tinyurl.com/RiptideSignup
Twitter: twitter.com/RiptideBooks
Facebook: facebook.com/RiptidePublishing
Goodreads: tinyurl.com/RiptideOnGoodreads
Tumblr: riptidepublishing.tumblr.com

Thank you so much for Reading the Rainbow!

RiptidePublishing.com

ABOUT
THE AUTHOR

A romance novelist and short story writer, Christine has over thirty publications to her name. She loves to exercise and stops writing just long enough to keep her body in motion too. When she's not pretending to be a ninja in her basement, she's most likely spending time with her family and two dogs.

Website: christinedabo.com
Twitter: @Christine_dAbo
Facebook: facebook.com/christine.dabo?ref=name
Instagram: instagram.com/christine.dabo
Tumblr: christinedabo.tumblr.com

Enjoy more stories like
Working It
at RiptidePublishing.com!

CPSIA information can be obtained
at www.ICGtesting.com
Printed in the USA
LVOW08s2312170317
527581LV00003B/94/P

9 781626 495227